Carla Cassidy is an award-winning, *New York Times* bestselling author who has written more than one hundred and twenty novels. Carla believes the only thing better than curling up with a good book to read is sitting down at the computer with a good story to write.

GUARDIAN COWBOY

CARLA CASSIDY

MILLS & BOON

First Published in Great Britain 2018
by Mills & Boon, an imprint of HarperCollins*Publishers*
1 London Bridge Street, London, SE1 9GF

Guardian Cowboy © 2018 Carla Bracale

ISBN: 978-0-263-26560-6

39-0218

MIX
Paper from
responsible sources
FSC™ C007454

This book is produced from independently certified FSC™
paper to ensure responsible forest management.

For more information visit: www.harpercollins.co.uk/green

Printed and bound in Spain
by CPI, Barcelona

Chapter 1

"If one of those cowboys from the Humes's ranch strokes my butt one more time, I'm going to toss a drink over somebody's head," Janis Little exclaimed to fellow Watering Hole waitress, Annie Holbrook, as they both reached the polished bar that stretched almost wall-to-wall along the side of the popular nightspot.

Annie grinned at her. "I double-dog dare you," she said, her dark eyes snapping with mischief. "Stroking butts is the only way those men can convince themselves they have any kind of a romantic relationship with a woman. I triple-dog dare you."

Janis laughed as the bartender, Tanner Woodson, approached them. "Ladies, talk to me," he said.

"Three draft beers," Annie said.

Janis gave him the orders for her tables and he stepped away to prepare the drinks.

"He is so hot," Annie whispered to Janis.

Tanner was not only new to the town of Bitterroot, Oklahoma, but tonight was only his third night on the job.

So far, as manager of the bar, Janis was impressed with him. He was friendly with the patrons but not overly so. He was quick and efficient, and when he had a moment to rest, he didn't. Instead he wiped down the bar, cleaned glasses and restocked the lemons and limes and olives that topped the drinks.

"Janis, did you hear what I said?" Annie poked Janis in the rib with her elbow.

"Yeah, he's okay," she replied.

"Okay? He's got the dreamiest blue eyes and that beautiful dark hair, and enough chest muscles to make a girl feel safe if she was in his arms."

"You're practically on the verge of drooling," Janis said dryly.

"You'd drool, too, if you weren't already hung up on that sexy Holiday Ranch cowboy who can't hold his drinks."

"I'm not hung up on anyone," Janis replied even as she felt her cheeks warm with a blush.

Thankfully, at that moment, Tanner returned with their drinks. The Watering Hole was the place for singles and dating couples to hang out and this evening it was hopping with the usual Saturday night crowd.

There was definitely one of the Holiday Ranch cowboys who made Janis's heart lift just a little bit whenever she saw him, but those men had yet to arrive for their ritual Saturday night of drinking and blowing off steam.

Right now she was stuck serving the Humes's ranch men, who seemed to live for the chance to make everyone else's life miserable. "Here we are," she said as she reached their table. She'd never met a group of more odious men.

"About time," Zeke Osmond said and then offered up a smarmy smile. "But I'll forgive you for taking so long if you give me a little kiss."

"Sorry, Zeke, I'm not allowed to kiss the customers."

It took her only a minute to serve the beers to Shep Harmon and Ace Sanders. Lloyd Green, the oldest of them all, got a Scotch on the rocks. As she bent over to place the drink in front of him, Zeke grabbed her butt.

She whirled around to face him, grabbed his beer from her tray and, with a pretend trip, poured every single drop into his lap.

"What the hell!" he shouted and jumped up out of his chair.

"Oh, I'm so sorry," she replied.

Lloyd guffawed. "Looks like you done peed your

pants, Zeke." The rest of the men at the table hooted with laughter.

"You did that on purpose." Zeke's dark eyes glittered with anger.

"It was an accident," she replied. "I'll go get you a bar towel so you can clean yourself up. I'll be right back."

As she headed to the bar, she shot a quick glance across the room. Annie grinned at her and flashed a quick thumbs-up sign.

It had been a highly unprofessional thing to do, but she wasn't sorry. She would do it again in a minute. She was tired of the Humes's men, and Zeke Osmond in particular, acting like it was their right to touch her body intimately.

"Tanner, can I get a clean towel?" she asked the bartender.

He reached down to a shelf under the bar and handed one to her. "Was that an accidentally-on-purpose move?" His blue eyes twinkled knowingly.

"I plead the fifth," she replied with a laugh.

She returned to the table and handed Zeke the towel. He was still standing, cursing and raving about her spilling the drink on purpose.

"Sit down and shut up already," Lloyd growled at him. "You're starting to give me a damned headache."

Zeke obeyed, settling back into his chair with the

towel in his lap and a glare at Janis. She ignored him and moved on to check on her other patrons.

At seven thirty the band began to play and people hit the wooden dance floor. The Croakin' Frogs, a local band, played every Saturday night. The rest of the nights the jukebox kept peoples' toes tapping.

It was just before eight when the men from the Holiday Ranch arrived. Although about a dozen worked on the ranch, only six came in the door, and one in particular made Janis's heart beat just a little bit faster.

Sawyer Quincy. He had ginger-colored hair and copper-hued eyes. His shoulders were broad enough to carry a woman into happily-ever-after and his jeans rode a little low on his slim hips. She'd had a silly crush on him for years.

The men greeted people as they wove their way through the crowded bar and settled in at one of the large booths in her section. As usual, Sawyer took the position in the corner of the booth where, before the night was over, he would slump down in a beer-induced unconsciousness. That man definitely shouldn't be drinking.

She approached the booth with her usual smile and her order pad ready.

"Ah, if it isn't our favorite waitress," Sawyer said. Although his smile made her feel like they shared something special, that was just the warmth he offered everyone with his gorgeous grins.

"And if it isn't my favorite group of men to wait on," she replied.

The Watering Hole served the usual bar fare like deep-fried pickles and mozzarella sticks, but the menu also offered up a variety of burgers and sandwiches. Within minutes, Janis had their drink and food orders and was headed to the kitchen to turn in her ticket.

She then served their drinks and returned to the kitchen to pick up their food.

"Busy night," Charlie Williams, the head cook, said to her.

"Saturday nights are always busy," she replied. "Maybe it would cut down on traffic if you didn't serve your famous pulled pork every Saturday."

"But then I wouldn't be worshipped as the barbecue king of Bitterroot," he joked and then sobered. "Still, tonight it seems like everyone in the place wants to eat." He looked over his shoulder. "Hey, Rusty, don't burn those fries." Charlie rolled his eyes at Janis and disappeared from the pass-through window.

As she waited, her gaze went across the room to Sawyer. He was laughing at something somebody had said. Even though right now she was too far away to actually hear him, she knew his laughter sounded like a deep, sexy melody.

She released a sigh. It was a silly crush because it was obvious Sawyer didn't look at her that way. She was Janis the waitress, just like Larry the mailman or Betty the bank clerk. He didn't really see her beyond her working role here in the bar.

"Janis, order up," Charlie called.

She grabbed one of the bigger food trays, loaded it with the cowboys' orders, and then went back to the booth to serve them.

The rest of the night passed like they all did. She served drinks and food, made lively chatter when necessary and pocketed the tips to add to the stash she hoped would one day be enough for a down payment on a nice little house.

For more years than she could count, she'd been living in the bar's back room. When Gary Runyon, the owner of the bar, had offered her not only a job but the opportunity to live rent-free in the bar's back room, she'd been thrilled. Before that, she'd been bunking with friends whenever possible and far too often sleeping in her car.

But she was soon going to be thirty years old and, while she loved what she did, she definitely wanted to make some changes in her life.

It was almost one in the morning when the place began to empty out, although the official closing time was two. As she approached the booth with the men from the Holiday Ranch, she saw that Sawyer was in his usual slumped position and totally out to the world.

She handed Flint McCay the tab for the table and

shook her head ruefully. "I don't know why that man drinks."

"He's definitely a lightweight," Clay Madison said, his blond hair gleaming in the light overhead.

"And if I remember right, it's your turn to take him home," Mac McBride said to Clay.

"No way, I took him in my truck last Saturday night," Clay protested.

"Well, I'm pretty sure it isn't my turn," Mac replied with a huff.

As the men argued about who would take the passed-out cowboy home and put him to bed, a plan quickly formulated in Janis's head.

You can't do that, a little voice whispered. *It would be too wicked. It's a totally crazy idea.*

But maybe it would prove a point with Sawyer. Maybe it would be exactly what he needed.

"Why don't you all carry him into the back room and put him in my bed?" she said before she could second-guess herself.

"For real?" Clay's blue eyes stared at her in surprise.

"For real," she replied. "I'd sure like to make him see that he's got a problem with his drinking. Maybe if he thinks he flirted with me all night and then wound up in my bed, he'll think twice about drinking himself into a stupor again."

"It's a great idea," Flint replied.

"A totally awesome idea," Clay agreed with a laugh.

Minutes later, the men had settled their tab and Sawyer had been carried into the back room Janis called home. The big, tall, cowboy didn't even blink an eye as they laid him in the middle of her lavender sheets.

Clay tossed Sawyer's brown hat onto one of the wooden posts of the four-poster bed.

"I'll see to it that he gets home in the morning," she said. "And this will be our little secret, at least for a day or two."

"Absolutely," Clay replied, his blue eyes sparkling with humor. "We won't say a word until you tell him the truth."

As they walked out into the bar area, regret instantly filled the back of her throat. Who did she think she was? Who was she to teach Sawyer Quincy any kind of a lesson?

Still, she hated the way the others made fun of him. From everything she'd heard, and from her own experience, she knew he was a terrific guy.

She suspected he had some kind of allergy to something in beer. There was nothing else to explain the fact that after two or three beers he completely passed out to the world.

Now it was too late to halt what she'd already put in motion. All the men had left and Sawyer was in her bed.

It was just after two when she locked up the bar

for the night and returned to her room to discover that he hadn't moved an inch.

It was a vision out of her wildest fantasies…only, in her fantasies, he was always conscious and gazing at her with adoring eyes.

She grabbed a nightgown out of one of her dresser drawers and headed into the small bathroom for a quick shower.

When she re-entered the bedroom, she knew exactly what she was going to do. It was definitely wicked—it was totally naughty—but she hoped to prove a point and, in doing so, she had to make it all look as real as possible.

She stood next to the bed and stared down at him. He had rugged features. His face was suntanned from the outside work he did and yet the fine lines that feathered outward from the corners of his eyes were definitely laugh lines. His eyelashes were thick and long, and a hint of whiskers darkened his lower, strong jaw.

Her gaze swept across his broad shoulders beneath his brown-plaid, button-up shirt. "In for a penny," she whispered to herself and then leaned over to unbutton his shirt.

She had it unfastened and had managed to maneuver one of his arms out of the sleeve when he mumbled something unintelligible.

She froze, her heart thumping madly. He immediately quieted again. She waited a minute and then drew in a deep breath and rolled him over to get the other arm out of the shirt.

She eyed the buttons on his jeans. Dare she? She had to. The only way this would really work was if he was out of his jeans.

Carefully, she unfastened them, thankful to see that he was wearing black briefs or boxers beneath. As she started to work the jeans down his body, he raised his hips to aid her.

"Thanks, Clay," he muttered.

She got the jeans down to his ankles and realized she hadn't taken off his boots. She tugged them off, along with his socks, and then dropped his jeans to the floor. She took out his wallet and placed it on the nightstand.

Lordy, lordy… A fully dressed Sawyer was sexy, but a nearly naked Sawyer wearing only a pair of black boxers and stretched out on her lavender sheets nearly stopped her heart.

She turned out the overhead light, leaving only the illumination from a night-light plugged into an outlet next to the bed. She fully admitted that she'd lost her ever-lovin' mind. But now she was fully committed to being temporarily insane.

Carefully, she crawled into bed, not touching him in any way. He smelled good, like minty soap, a woodsy cologne and a hint of beer.

Even though she wasn't touching him, his body

heat warmed her in a delicious way and she fought the impulse to lean into him.

As she closed her eyes, she wished this was for real. She wished Sawyer Quincy was in her bed because he wanted to be, because he had chosen to be with her out of all the women in Bitterroot.

Consciousness came to Sawyer in bits and pieces. The first thing he noticed was that the sheets smelled like flowers. With his eyes still closed, he frowned, wondering how flowers had gotten into his bed.

Of course it wouldn't be the first time he'd awakened after a Saturday night of drinking to find something strange in his bed. The other men were real jokesters and in the past he'd awakened to discover he was sharing the bed with a salami sandwich, a dead fish, a prickly tumbleweed and his saddle, just to name a few.

He cracked open an eyelid to the early morning sun drifting through a window…not his window. He'd never seen that window before with its frilly white curtains. Where in the hell was he? With both eyes wide open, the next thing he noted was that he was in a four-poster bed with purple sheets. His hat hung on one of the posters, as if it belonged there.

He turned over and nearly jumped out of the bed. A woman…in the bed…with him… Who was she? She faced away from him and all he could see was short, thick, dark hair and creamy bare shoulders beneath hot-pink spaghetti straps.

His shock forced a loud gasp from his throat. He remained frozen in surprise as the woman rolled over, shoved the hair away from her face and gave him a sleepy, sexy smile.

"Good morning, lover," she said.

Lover… Janis? His brain short-circuited. Hell's bells, what had he done last night?

"Uh…good morning," he managed to reply.

He tensed as she snuggled up against him. Of their own volition, his arms went around her. Her silky nightgown was a poor barrier, as he could feel not only the heat of her breasts against him but also the hint of taut nipples.

"Last night was the most wonderful night of my life," she murmured into the hollow of his neck. "You're the best, Sawyer. You made my whole body sing with pleasure."

"Yeah, uh, likewise." As hard as he tried, he couldn't remember what had happened between them that had gotten them here in her bed. The last thing he did remember was her serving him a third beer.

His impulse was to grab his boots and britches and run like hell out the door. However, his mother had raised him better than that. But he definitely didn't want to hang around and chat long enough for her to realize he had no memory of making her sing with pleasure. He'd always liked Janis and the last thing he'd want to do was to hurt her feelings.

Despite his shock at the position he found himself in, his body began to respond to her closeness. Thankfully, at that moment, she rolled away from him and sat up. "How about I fix you a nice, big breakfast? You more than earned it after last night."

Had her eyes always been that inviting shade of caramel? Had her dark eyelashes always been so long? He'd never noticed before now. He quickly averted his gaze and looked around the room. There wasn't much to look at and certainly no kitchen anywhere in sight.

"You seem to be missing some important things... like a stove and a refrigerator." He frantically continued to search his mind for any memory from the night before.

He usually just passed out when he drank, but he had suffered a couple of blackouts in the past. Once he'd found himself sleeping in the pasture next to the pond after the other men had insisted they'd put him in his own bed. Another time he'd planted himself in Mac's room and had sung all the country-western songs he'd ever known. The next day he'd had no memory of it.

"I have all the equipment I need just outside that door," she said. He knew she was referring to the bar's kitchen.

She scooted off the bed and Sawyer averted his gaze once again, but not before he caught a glimpse of long, shapely, bare legs beneath her hot-pink nightie.

"I'll be right back and we can talk about breakfast." She disappeared through a door he assumed led to a bathroom.

The minute the door closed behind her, he leaped out of bed. He searched frantically on the floor for his jeans and shirt. When he found them, he dressed as quickly as possible. No matter what had happened between them the night before, he wasn't comfortable being nearly naked in her bed.

He needed to get out...to get away and process the night he couldn't remember. How did this change things? What were the consequences? It was obvious she was thrilled with whatever had occurred.

You're the best, Sawyer. You made my whole body sing with pleasure.

Her words echoed in his brain as he pulled on his boots. At least she'd been pleased with his performance, he thought with a touch of pride.

The pride didn't last long. In truth, he was ashamed. He grabbed his wallet off the nightstand and opened it, frowning as he saw the condom he carried still in place. Oh, crap, they hadn't even had protected sex.

His mama would be rolling around in her grave

knowing that he'd gotten drunk and taken some random woman to bed.

Only, Janis wasn't exactly random. He'd always found her pleasant and pretty. He'd just never thought of her *that* way before. Geez, what had he done?

He grabbed his cell phone out of his jeans' pocket and dialed the number for Clay. Clay had a reputation as a womanizer. He'd know what to do in this situation.

He released a sigh of relief as Clay answered.

"Come get me," Sawyer said without preamble.

Clay laughed. "What's the matter, bro? Having a rough morning after?"

"Just come and pick me up behind the bar."

Sawyer had just pocketed his cell phone when Janis stepped out of the bathroom. He swallowed hard. He'd thought she was in there getting dressed, but the only thing she had done was pull a short, silky robe over the sexy nightie.

"Oh, you're already dressed," she said. "So I guess you don't want breakfast in bed."

"Uh, no, but thanks anyway. I just called Clay to come and get me. I need to get back to the ranch."

"I would have taken you home," she protested. "I can at least make you a cup of coffee before you go." She smiled at him and motioned to a small table that held one of those fancy coffeemakers that gave up a cup of coffee in seconds. Next to the machine were a couple of cups, a sugar bowl and several little creamers.

"That would be nice," he agreed and sat on the very edge of the bed. He just hoped she didn't want to chew over the details about the night before.

As she put the little pod into place, he couldn't help but notice her sexy long legs. This was a Janis he didn't know. She was so far removed from the efficient, jeans-clad woman who served him drinks on Saturday nights.

And apparently he'd made love with her last night.

He needed to get out of there and have some time to process everything. It was hard to think with her in the same small room, looking so soft and gorgeous and smelling like fresh flowers.

"Cream or sugar?" she asked once the coffee machine had whooshed the last of the liquid into the cup.

"No, thanks. Black is fine," he replied as he took the cup from her.

She made herself a cup and sat on the opposite side of the bed. "You know, Sawyer, I've had a crush on you for a long time. I'm so glad last night you let me know you felt the same way about me."

He had? Some of the other guys had teased him about having a crush on Janis, but that was just because he'd mentioned in passing a couple of times that he thought she was pretty.

"Yeah, me, too," he replied because he didn't know what else to say.

"So, when will I see you again?"

"Uh, maybe we could have dinner at the café some time," he replied and then nervously took a sip of coffee.

"The bar is closed tonight, so I'm free."

Oh, her eyes held almost as much heat as the cup in his hand. "Okay. Then how about I pick you up around six?"

"That would be perfect," she replied with a smile.

A horn honked from outside and he jumped up so fast from the bed he sloshed some of the coffee onto his fingers. "That will be Clay."

She took his cup from him and set both his and hers on the little table. Together, they walked over to the door that led outside.

She opened it and then she was in his arms, her face raised for a kiss. He didn't deny her. He wrapped his arms around her and lowered his mouth to hers. Her lips were invitingly soft and hot. Instantly, a fire of hunger leaped into his veins.

He couldn't believe that he had no memories of kissing her last night. Before he followed through on his desire to deepen the kiss, he dropped his arms and stepped back. "I'll see you at six tonight," he said.

"I'll be waiting," she replied.

Sawyer practically ran for Clay's truck. He got in

on the passenger side and turned to the blond-haired driver. "Clay, you've got to help me out, man. I guess I did something crazy last night and I don't remember it and now I'm in way over my head."

Clay released a dry chuckle. "Welcome to the world of drunk adulting."

Chapter 2

Janis couldn't help the bouts of laughter that overtook her throughout the course of the day. Each time she thought of the stunned look on Sawyer's face when he'd first awakened, she got the giggles.

His copper-colored eyes had radiated a quiet panic as he'd maneuvered the morning conversation in a way for her not to know he had no memory of them having sex.

Of course he had no memory. Absolutely nothing had happened between them. He had slept soundly through the night while sleep had remained elusive for her because she'd been so acutely aware of him next to her in the bed.

His scent had surrounded her and she'd tried to

match her breathing to his. She'd wondered what it would really be like to make love with him.

What she'd done to him was wrong on so many levels, but, if given the same opportunity, she would do it again. What if another woman had gotten him to go home with her while he'd been blindly drunk?

It would be easy to lift his wallet or to make him believe he was a baby daddy or to kill him when he was in that kind of condition.

No hint of laughter left her lips as she thought of all the bad things that could happen to him. He was lucky his fellow cowboys babysat him when he passed out. But he was a grown man and shouldn't have to rely on the kindness of others to see him home safe and sound.

She'd tell him the truth tonight over dinner. She had no idea how he would react. It was possible her little ploy would make him so angry he'd never speak to her again. Hopefully, he'd take it all in good humor and see that the intent behind it was good and she'd meant him no harm.

Still, her heart raced as she dressed for the evening out. Was it beating more frantically because she didn't know what to expect from him when she told him the truth? Or was the quickened rhythm because she was finally going to spend some quality time with the man she'd had an interest in for so long?

Dinner at the café wasn't exactly a formal affair, so she pulled on a pair of jeans and topped them with a coral-colored sweater she knew complemented her chin-length brown hair and brown eyes.

At five to six that evening she stood at the window next to the door with her coat in hand. March had definitely roared in like a lion, hanging on to the cold and blustery winds of winter.

She was ready for spring, with warm breezes and the scent of new grass and flowers in the air. A smile touched her lips as a memory of her father jumped into her mind.

Her father had loved spring, too. One day, when she was about ten years old, he'd pulled her out of the house and onto the front lawn. Together they had stretched out on the ground. "Listen," he'd said.

"What am I listening to?" she'd asked.

"The earth's heartbeat," he'd replied. "Sometimes it's just nice to be quiet and listen."

A sharp pain of grief pierced through her heart. Her dad had died of a heart attack when Janis was sixteen. That was the day every ounce of love had been taken from Janis's world.

The pain was vanquished by the sight of Sawyer's truck pulling into the small parking lot.

Her heart began to beat with the anticipation and excitement of the evening to come in his company.

Before he could get out of the truck, she pulled on her coat and stepped outside the door. She ran to the passenger door and got in.

"Hi," she greeted cheerfully.

"Hi, yourself," he replied. "You know, I would have walked up to your door to get you like a proper gentleman if you hadn't run out so quickly." He pulled out of the parking area behind the bar and onto Main Street.

"There was no reason for you to get out in the cold," she replied. The interior of the truck smelled pleasant and masculine, with hints of rich leather and his woodsy cologne.

"Are you hungry?" he asked.

"I'm starving. What about you?"

"I can always eat, but tonight was a good night to head to the café instead of eating at the ranch. Cookie made meatloaf and I'm not particularly partial to it."

"What's your favorite meal?"

She noted how his stiff shoulders began to relax as the conversation remained light and easy. The poor man was probably afraid she was going to bring up last night. She didn't intend to even mention it until the end of this night when she'd tell him the truth.

"As far as I'm concerned, there's nothing better than a big, juicy cheeseburger. What about you?"

"French fries. I like them plain or smothered with cheese or covered with chili."

He laughed and flashed her a quick glance. "That's not a real meal."

"Bet me," she replied, making him laugh once again.

By that time they'd arrived at the Bitterroot Café.

Sundays, the place was usually packed at lunchtime, after church services let out. But on Sunday evenings there were not too many diners.

Janis was glad. It would make conversation easier. She knew she was intensely physically attracted to Sawyer, but she also recognized that she didn't know that much about him. By the end of this meal, her attraction to him just might be dead.

Amanda Wright greeted them as they walked in. A month ago, she'd bought the café from Daisy Martin, a fiery redhead who had owned it for as long as anyone could remember.

Janis knew that wasn't the only change that had occurred in Mandy's life. A month and a half ago, after a whirlwind romance, she and Brody Booth had run off to Las Vegas and gotten married.

"Lately it seems like weddings are in the air in Bitterroot," Janis said once they were seated in a booth and had shrugged out of their coats.

Sawyer's gaze turned wary and she couldn't help but laugh. "Don't worry, Sawyer, shotgun weddings went out of style a long time ago. Besides, I don't have a big brother or a daddy to come after you."

He visibly relaxed. "But isn't June Little, who works at the mercantile, your mother?"

It was Janis's turn to stiffen slightly. "She is, but I don't have any kind of a relationship with her right now."

"That's a shame," he replied.

Before the conversation could go any further, Carlie Martin appeared to take their orders.

"How's it going, Carlie?" Janis asked the pretty blond waitress.

"It's going," she replied. "We had a hellacious crowd in for lunch but, thankfully, it's been a fairly slow night, so we've all managed to catch our breaths."

After a little more small talk, Sawyer ordered a burger and fries. Janis opted for a chicken and bacon wrap, a new item on the menu, and a side of fries.

"Tell me why you don't have a relationship with your mother?" he asked once Carlie had left the booth.

"Oh, it's a long, boring story. I'd much rather hear about you," she replied. "Through the years I've heard so many rumors about all you men on the Holiday Ranch."

He grinned. "Probably at least half of them aren't true."

She could listen to the sound of his deep laughter forever. "So, you weren't all found under lily pads in Big Cass's pond." She'd wanted him to laugh again and she was successful.

"No," he replied, a sparkle of humor in his eyes. "And we weren't all brought in from a reform school when we were kids. But we were all runaways or throwaways who took to the streets when we were young."

"And which one were you? A runaway or a throw-away?"

"A runaway," he replied.

"Why?" These were the kinds of things she wanted to know. Who he was as a man, where he'd come from, and what forces might be at play in his life that made him drink himself into a stupor on most Saturday nights when he came into the bar.

He looked so sexy tonight in his jeans and a rust-colored shirt that matched his slightly unruly hair and stretched across his broad shoulders.

"Unlike a lot of the other men who suffered from mental and physical abuse, I ran away when my mom died because I didn't want to go into foster care." He gave a dry chuckle. "At fifteen years old, I thought I was old enough and strong enough to survive on my own. But if it hadn't been for Cass Holiday and Francine Rogers, I probably would have died on the streets or wound up in jail."

"Who is Francine Rogers?" Everyone in town had known Big Cass Holiday, who had died a year ago in a tornado.

"She was a social worker and a good friend of Cass's. She worked the streets at night in Oklahoma City. She tried to reunite kids with their parents, if possible. She's the one responsible for getting us all off the streets and working for Cass. Unfortunately we heard Francine passed away a couple of months ago."

The conversation was interrupted by the arrival of their orders. "Anything else I can get you?" Carlie asked once she had placed their plates in front of them.

"I think we're good," Sawyer replied. When she left, Sawyer looked at Janis, his eyes lit with curiosity. "Now, tell me about you. I know you've worked at the bar for a long time, but I don't know much about your personal life."

"That's because I don't have much of a personal life," she replied ruefully as she dragged one of her fries through a puddle of ketchup. "I live at the bar. I work at the bar. And that's about the sum of it."

"What do you do for fun?"

"I love to read and sometimes I just like to drive out into the country and sit and listen to the soft noise of nature at work." A blush warmed her cheeks. "I know it probably sounds silly."

"It doesn't sound silly at all to me," he replied. "Living with eleven other rowdy cowboys, sometimes I just need to get away and enjoy the sounds of nature. When that happens, I usually grab my fishing pole and head down to the pond."

"That sounds like fun," she replied.

"Maybe on a warm day I'll take you to the pond with me."

Her heart swelled at his words. "That would be nice," she said. But once she told him the truth about the night before, he might be so angry he wouldn't be speaking to her tomorrow or on the next warm day.

For the next hour they ate and talked and laughed. Sawyer seemed to be the man she'd thought he would be…easygoing, easy to talk to, and with a great sense of humor.

She loved the way his eyes shone when he talked about his work at the ranch and the other ranch hands, who were like brothers to him. She also liked that he was fiercely loyal to Cassie Bowie, who was Big Cass's niece and had taken over the ranch after Cass had died.

It would be easy to allow her crush on him to blossom into something more, but first Janis had to tell him the truth.

She'd tell him at her doorstep, she thought. That way, if he was really angry with her, at least she'd already be home. Besides, she wasn't ready for this pleasant time with him to end yet.

"Are you a dessert kind of girl?" he asked when they'd finished the meal.

"I wouldn't turn up my nose at a piece of chocolate cake," she replied.

"Then the lady shall eat cake," he replied and gestured to get Carlie's attention.

"I hope the lady won't be eating cake all alone?"

He grinned at her. "I can't walk out of here without eating a piece of Mandy's fancy crème brûlée cake."

"I noticed it was a new item on the menu. I'm assuming it's good?"

His eyes warmed and a sensual curl of his lips shot heat through her. "It's good enough to make a grown man weep," he replied.

Oh, my, but she'd love for him to look that way, to talk that way, about her.

They had just been served their desserts and coffee when Tony Nakni, his wife, Mary, and Mary's grandmother, Halena, came in.

Tony and Mary waved as they took a booth on the opposite side of the café, while Halena wove her way through the tables in the center to approach Janis and Sawyer.

"Hi, Halena," Janis said.

Halena Redwing was one of the more colorful characters in Bitterroot. She had the proud, beautiful, facial features of her Choctaw blood and a mischievous twinkle in her dark eyes. Rumor had it she loved dancing naked in rainstorms. She also had a penchant for funky hats and evening dresses.

Tonight she was clad in a red gown with glittery matching shoes. A little hat of black-and-red feathers sat atop her shiny silver hair.

"Evening, ma'am," Sawyer said.

"Sawyer, it's nice to see you out with a good woman," Halena said. "It's past time for you to get married and have a bunch of babies."

"Halena." Janis laughed. "We're just having dinner," she protested.

"Dinner is a good start and you could do a lot worse." Halena leaned into Janis. "He's got the sexiest, most pinchable butt in all of Bitterroot," she said in a loud, mock whisper.

"Geez, Halena." Sawyer's cheeks flushed red.

"Just saying," she said and then turned on her sparkly red shoes and headed back to the booth where Tony and Mary awaited her.

"Halena is definitely a pip," Janis said.

"I swear that woman likes to torment me whenever she sees me," Sawyer said, but his voice held a wealth of affection. "She steals my hat whenever she can and goes out of her way to embarrass me whenever possible."

"At least she gave me some valuable information." Janis grinned at him teasingly.

Once again Sawyer's cheeks dusted with color. "And now would be a great time to change the subject."

They lingered over coffee and their conversation remained light and easy.

"Favorite music?" he asked her.

"Anything country," she replied.

"Favorite flower?"

"Pink roses. When I went to my first school dance, my date didn't know he was supposed to get me a corsage. My dad ran to the florist and got me a beautiful corsage of pink roses. They remind me of love."

"Favorite place to hang out in Bitterroot?"

She frowned thoughtfully. "The courtyard in the center of town is a nice place to sit and relax."

Then it was her turn to fire questions at him. She learned that spring was his favorite season and he loved the sound of a redbird's song. His favorite time of day was evening and he'd broken his arm when the other guys had dared him to ride a bull named Cowboy Crusher.

They spent a half hour firing all kinds of questions to each other. She was disappointed when their cups were empty and it was time to leave. But she knew work time came early for him at the ranch.

As she got into his truck, nervous butterflies took flight in the pit of her stomach. Now was the time of reckoning. She had to tell him that nothing had happened between them last night.

"This has been nice," he said when they were a block away from the bar. "I feel like we sort of jumped the gun last night and now we need to work backward and get to know each other better."

She gazed at him in the illumination of the dashboard. "Sawyer…about last night," she began. She turned her gaze out the front window, unable to look at him while she made her confession. As his headlights splashed across the back of the bar, she gasped in horror.

* * *

Sawyer stared at the white paint sprayed across the dark wood of the building. The letters were huge—Janis Little is a Whore.

What the hell? Was this because of what had happened last night? Who else had known that he'd spent the night in her bed besides a couple of his friends?

Janis began to cry. "Oh, my God…wh-who would do this?" she said between her gulping sobs. "I… I'm not a whore. I'm not."

She turned to look at him and in her eyes he saw not only shock and hurt, but also a fierce denial of the characterization the words gave her.

"Janis, of course you're not…" he began in an attempt to calm her down. He turned off his headlights so the words were no longer visible in the darkness of the night.

"I've only had one lover in my whole life. Only one, and I'm thirty years old. You're the one and only man who has ever stayed in my room overnight. I wasn't a whore when I was growing up and I'm not a whore now." Anything else she might have had to say was made impossible as she buried her face in her hands and wept in earnest.

"Janis, nobody believes you're a whore," he said. "I mean, nobody I know believes that." It was true. He had never heard any hint or whisper of a rumor about Janis being loose and wild. "This is the work of some no-count creep. Don't worry, I'll make sure it's cleaned up before morning, but first we need to call Dillon."

Dillon Bowie was the chief of police for the small town. More recently he had become the husband of Cassie, who owned the ranch Sawyer called home.

"And I should call Gary," she said as she drew in several deep breaths in an obvious effort to push back her tears.

Gary Runyon owned the bar and Sawyer agreed that he should be called, as well.

The minute the calls had been made, Janis got out of the truck. Sawyer quickly followed her. She stood with her back to him and stared at the building where the letters were faintly visible in the illumination from a nearby streetlight.

He could hear that she was still softly crying and could see that her entire body visibly trembled. "Janis," he said softly as he grabbed her by one arm and turned her around to face him.

She instantly came into his arms and buried her face in the crook of his neck. He wrapped his arms around her in an effort to somehow comfort her.

"Nobody will see this except us and Dillon and Gary," he said. "I'll make sure it's painted over by morning. I promise."

"But why would somebody do this to me?" Her breath was a warm caress against his neck. She re-leased a small laugh that had nothing to do with her being amused. "If I didn't know better, I'd think my mother was behind this."

"Your mother?" Shock swept through him.

She shook her head. "Never mind. Like I said earlier, it's a long story for another time."

What kind of story could make a woman believe her mother was capable of doing something like this? Sawyer couldn't imagine. "Come on, let's get back in the truck to wait. It's cold out here."

They got back in the truck, where he started the engine to get some heat blowing from the vents.

"I'm sorry, Janis," he said.

She turned and looked at him in surprise. "Why are you sorry?"

"I feel partially responsible for this. It probably wouldn't have happened if I hadn't spent the night with you last night."

"I'm a grown woman and I have a right to a personal life without somebody judging me for it. This is just so embarrassing…and…and it's vile. I hope Dillon finds the person responsible," she replied.

Sawyer didn't want to tell her that he seriously doubted Dillon would be able to catch the culprit. In any case, at that moment Dillon arrived, his lights whirling blue and red across the building.

Sawyer and Janis got out of the truck as Dillon departed his police car. "Nasty piece of work," he said in greeting. He looked at Janis. "Any idea who might be responsible?"

She shook her head. "None. I can't imagine who would do something like this."

"I, uh… I spent the night with Janis last night," Sawyer said. "Maybe that has something to do with it?"

"Janis's business should be nobody else's business," Dillon replied. "You're both consenting adults."

"Wait…maybe I do know somebody who would do something like this. Last night at work I poured a beer in Zeke Osmond's lap," Janis said.

"Was it an accident or on-purpose spill?" Dillon asked.

"On purpose," she replied. "He kept grabbing my backside and I'd finally had enough." Her gaze went back to the building. "He was definitely angry enough at me to do something like this."

"Or maybe you have a secret admirer who didn't like the idea of you being with Sawyer," Dillon said in speculation. "I'm going to look around to see if I can find a paint can that might have been discarded. But, honestly, there isn't much I can do about this."

Gary Runyon's van pulled into the parking lot. Gary was a big man, with broad shoulders and a barrel chest. He and his wife, Abigail, had recently celebrated their twenty-seventh wedding anniversary. They had two daughters.

"Gary, I'm so sorry," Janis said. "Please don't let me go."

"Let you go? You mean fire you?" He shook his

head. "Janis, honey, did you paint the back of my building?" he asked.

"Of course not," she replied.

"Then why on earth would I let you go? You're the best damned bar manager anyone could have." The big man nodded at Sawyer and then walked over to Dillon, who had begun his paint can hunt.

Sawyer flung an arm over Janis's shoulder. "You okay?" he asked.

"As okay as I can be," she replied as she moved even closer to his side. She looked over to where Dillon was walking around and Gary was on his cell phone. "Dillon isn't going to be able to find out who did this, is he?"

Sawyer hesitated a moment and then replied, "Probably not. But somebody who has the mentality to do something like this will possibly brag to a friend, or get drunk and say something incriminating. Zeke Osmond isn't the brightest star in the sky."

Gary walked over to where the two of them stood. "I've called in Miguel and James to repaint the building. They should be arriving within the next half hour or so." He smiled at Janis. "Don't you worry, honey. This will all be gone well before morning."

Sawyer knew both men in passing and they had always been friendly. Miguel Gomez was one of the cooks and James Warner worked as the bar's janitor.

"Dock my pay," Janis said. "I know those two will

expect to be paid for working on something like this in the middle of the night."

"Don't you worry about it. I've got this," Gary replied. "Why don't you get out of the cold and get inside where you belong?"

She took Gary's advice.

Minutes later she sat on the bed inside her room with Sawyer seated next to her. They had taken off their coats and hung them on hooks on the wall next to the door. "You sure know how to make a date exciting," Sawyer said in an effort to lift the darkness from her eyes.

She gave him a small smile. "I like a little excitement on my dates, but not quite this much." The smile lasted only a minute and then fell away. "Sawyer, you don't have to stay any longer. I'm fine."

"I just thought I'd hang around until Miguel and James show up to get things cleaned up and then I'll head home." He wanted to ask her about her mother. He also wanted to know if she always smelled so good and if he'd really been a good lover the night before. But now wasn't the time or the place for those kinds of conversations.

"At least I can thank you for a wonderful evening before you brought me home," she said. She wiped at her cheeks. "And I suppose I look like a raccoon now from all my blubbering."

"A very pretty raccoon," he replied. It was true that some of her mascara now rested beneath her eyes where it didn't belong, but even that didn't detract from her natural prettiness.

Unexpected desire surged inside him and he got up from the bed. "Do you want me to make you a cup of coffee before I leave?" He gestured to the machine she'd used that morning to make him a cup of brew. "Although I imagine you could probably use something stronger."

"I don't drink alcohol."

He looked at her in surprise. "You work here and you don't drink?"

"Maybe it's because I do work here that I don't," she replied. "I've seen a lot of people act the fool because of too much alcohol and it's just really never interested me."

A wave of uncomfortable guilt swept through him. He was one of those fools. He'd been so foolish last night he'd made love to a beautiful woman and had been so addled by alcohol he didn't even remember it.

Before they could say another word, a knock sounded on her door. It was Gary letting her know the men had arrived and were already at work on painting over the ugly words.

"Are you sure you'll be okay?" Sawyer asked as he grabbed his coat from the hook.

"I'll be just fine. Go on and get out of here. I know you have early mornings on the ranch." She got up and joined him at the door.

"Janis, don't let this get to you." Anger on her behalf suddenly rose up to course through his veins. "If I find out who did this, I'll beat their hide clear out of town."

"My hero," she replied with a smile.

It was a smile that stirred a hunger for her inside him and told him it was time to leave. "I'll talk to you tomorrow." He was about to open the door to exit when she said his name and stopped him.

She gazed at him for a long moment and then shook her head. "Never mind. Good night."

He walked outside to see the two men painting over the spray-painted words. They nodded to him and kept working. He got into his truck and pulled away, his thoughts in chaos.

Who all had known he'd gone into the back room last night with Janis and had spent the night there? The cowboys from the Holiday Ranch would have known because they hadn't had to get him home and into his bunkroom. There was no way any of them would have done something like this.

But you thought you knew Adam and he turned out to be a serial killer, a little voice reminded him.

He clenched his hands a little tighter around the steering wheel as he thought about Adam Benson.

Adam had been one of the lost boys who had wound up at the ranch with the others. Sawyer had grown up with the man, worked side-by-side with him and had never seen a hint of the monster hiding inside the man.

It wasn't until Adam had decided in his sick mind that Cassie had to die that all his crimes were uncovered. Thankfully, Dillon had shot Adam just before he'd killed Cassie with an ax. Adam had not only tried to kill Cassie, he'd also killed a new hire at the ranch.

But most horrifying of all was the discovery that, years ago, he'd killed seven teenagers because he hadn't thought they were good enough to work for Big Cass Holiday.

So, was one of his "brothers" hiding a dark side? Did one of them have a secret crush on Janis and had spray-painted the building because she'd hooked up with Sawyer? He just had trouble believing that of any one of them.

So, who else had been in the bar at closing time to know?

It was definitely possible Zeke Osmond had done it as a childish attempt to get revenge on Janis for dumping a beer on him. That would be in keeping with the nasty personality of the man.

Zeke worked on the Humes's ranch next to the Holiday property. All the men who worked for Raymond Humes shared the common trait of being nasty troublemakers. The bad blood between the Humes and the Holiday Ranch cowboys was the stuff of legend.

If Zeke was responsible for this, Sawyer would have no problem taking him to the woodshed, so to speak. No man should do something like this to a woman...ever.

He could only imagine the gossip that would have fired through the small town if morning had come and the spray-painted words had been seen by everyone. Bitterroot was a place that loved its gossip.

He didn't know who was responsible and he was confused about his feelings toward Janis.

Normally, Sawyer was a man who took his time when it came to romancing a woman. Sometimes he took so long the woman lost interest. But he intended to only be married once, so it was important that he got it right.

Lately he'd been thinking a lot about love and marriage. Maybe it was because so many of his friends had gotten hitched in the past year. And he wanted children. He wanted to be the kind of father he used to dream about having as a little boy.

Was Janis his forever woman? He had no idea. Everything had happened so fast with her. He'd invited her out to dinner because he'd felt obligated after the night before.

But he'd enjoyed her company throughout the evening. He'd noticed that she was pretty before, but having her all to himself instead of seeing her in the bar had been surprisingly exciting.

Something about the sparkle in her caramel-brown eyes drew him in. Her smile and her easy laughter were more than a little bit sexy. There was no question he was attracted to her in a way he hadn't been before.

And he'd already slept with her and didn't remember it.

When he reached the Holiday Ranch, he pulled his truck into the oversize shed that held all the cowboys' personal vehicles. In the distance was the big, two-story house where Cassie and Dillon lived. In the opposite direction was the bunkhouse.

The bunkhouse was set up like a motel with twelve small units that housed each of the men. At the back of the building was the dining and rec room. Cord Cully, aka Cookie, provided three meals a day for the ranch hands.

It had been in the dining room that Cassie and Dillon had gotten married on Valentine's Day. All the cowboys and their wives and girlfriends had been invited. Sawyer had attended the event alone.

Janis was right. Love and marriage had definitely been in the air in Bitterroot over the past several months. Maybe that's what had Sawyer thinking more and more about marriage.

He entered his bunk and tossed his hat on the bed. The room was small, with a single bed against one wall and a chest of drawers on the other. There was a closet and an adjoining bathroom. The only things decorating the walls were pictures of Sawyer with his mother that he'd taken with him on the night he'd run away.

He sank down onto the edge of the bed and dragged a hand through his hair. *Janis Little is a whore.* Yes, it was very possible Zeke had done it, a bit of childish revenge for a dropped drink. Hopefully this would be the end of it.

But if it wasn't Zeke, then who in the hell would do such a terrible thing?

Chapter 3

It was almost noon before Janis pulled herself up and out of bed the next day. She'd been up late listening to Miguel and James work outside.

There was no way to describe the shock and horror of the night before. Of all the things that could have been painted on the building, the word "whore" had taken her back to some very painful teenage years. Years that she preferred to not think about ever again for the rest of her life.

She now made herself a cup of coffee and then sat on the chair on one side of the bed to drink it. Aside from the horrifying discovery at the end of the night, she'd thoroughly enjoyed her time with Sawyer.

Physically, she was very drawn to him. The copper of his eyes was both warm and a bit unusual. His cinnamon-colored hair was a bit too long and with more than a hint of curl. It begged for fingers to dance through the thick strands. His face was all interesting lines and angles weathered to a beautiful bronze and he had a smile that warmed everyone in proximity.

She had also thoroughly enjoyed their conversation. She'd found him both intelligent and fun. Smart and with a good sense of humor, it was a heady combination in a man.

Oh, yes, she was definitely drawn to him. But she doubted she would hear from him again unless it was on a Saturday night when he came into the bar with his buddies for drinks.

Who would want to be with a woman somebody had called a whore? Why on earth would he want to get involved in this kind of drama? And, as if being called a whore wasn't bad enough, he thought she'd fallen into bed with him without having any kind of a real relationship with him at all.

She'd wanted to tell him the truth last night, but everything had ended on such a bad note, she hadn't gotten it done. And she needed to tell him. If nothing else, so that he knew she wasn't the kind of woman to just fall in bed with a random guy.

She shoved away thoughts of Sawyer, finished her coffee and went into the bathroom for a long shower. Her work schedule today was from three to closing time at midnight. The bar was open until midnight Mondays through Thursdays, and then stayed open until two on Fridays and Saturday nights. The place opened at eleven thirty every day.

Sundays, the bar was closed and Janis usually had the day off on Thursdays. However, she intended to talk to Gary about working without pay for the next couple of Thursdays to pay back whatever he'd had to give the men who had painted the building the night before.

She dressed in the T-shirt that advertised the bar across the chest and jeans that were her usual uniform. She then turned on the small television on the dresser in an effort to find something to take her mind off Sawyer and the horrible spray-painted message.

At least the weather report was for a nice spring warm-up over the next few days. Everyone would welcome nicer temperatures without the blustery wind.

By three o'clock she was more than ready to go to work. She was sick of her own brooding and ready to visit with the patrons who came in.

The minute she entered the bar proper, Annie rushed over to her. "Guess what I heard?" she asked.

Every one of Janis's stomach muscles instantly tightened. Oh, God, had somebody seen the spray paint before it was covered? Was she now the topic of all kinds of rumors and speculation around town?

"What did you hear?" she asked, holding her breath to wait for the answer.

"I heard that a certain woman was seen having dinner with a hot cowboy last night. I want all the details."

Janis laughed with more than a little bit of relief. "First, I want to know how you heard about it."

"You know my grandmother is good friends with Halena, who told her this morning while they had coffee together, and then my grandmother told me. Now…details please."

"I had the chicken wrap with french fries and Sawyer had a burger and fries," she told her. "Then we both had dessert and coffee."

"Don't make me slap you upside the head," Annie replied. "You know that's not what I care about. Did you like him? Did he like you? Are you going to see him again? Did he kiss you?" The words tumbled out of Annie's mouth in usual Annie style.

"I like him. I don't know if he likes me. I don't know if I'll see him again. And it's none of your business if he kissed me."

Annie's eyes sparkled. "So, he did kiss you! Was it a sweet kiss or a hot, tongue-and-all kiss?"

"Annie, stop," Janis replied with more laughter. She could always count on her friend to pull her out of the doldrums. Annie was unfailingly cheerful and truly interested in everything and everyone. "It was just dinner out…no big deal."

"I know you've had a crush on him forever, so him asking you out is a very big deal," Annie stated. "Who suggested dessert? Him or you?"

"He did."

"That's awesome. That means he likes you and wanted to spend a little more time with you," Annie proclaimed.

"And I'm sure some of the customers around here would like the two of us to quit chatting and get to work," Janis replied.

"I hate it when you act like the manager of this place," Annie said with a fake pout.

"Do I need to remind you that I am the manager of this place?" Janis laughed as Annie danced away to the section she'd be working that day.

Janis greeted Chance Aldrich, who worked as their part-time bartender. He had a ranch on the outskirts of town, but Janis guessed things weren't going too well there for him to have to pick up extra money bartending.

There were several people already in their usual places in the bar. Lester Caldwell, one of the grumpiest old men in Bitterroot, sat at the bar, nursing a whiskey. Lester complained about the drinks, the food and the music, yet he sat on the same stool every afternoon from about three to five.

Myles Hennessy was also a regular. A pleasant man in his late fifties, he shamelessly flirted with the waitresses and loved the bar's pulled pork sandwiches with fried pickles.

For the most part Janis enjoyed the people who frequented the bar. It was only occasionally, on a busy Friday or Saturday night, that too much alcohol combined with too much testosterone and a fight ensued.

"Hi, Lester," she said as she greeted the old man. "Can I get you a fresh one?" She gestured to the empty glass before him.

"Okay, but don't water it down none. I swear every drink I get in this place is watered down to profit the bar," he grumbled.

She knew there was no reason to waste her breath explaining to him that if he wanted a whiskey on the rocks and nursed it for over an hour, the odds were good the ice cubes would melt and water down the alcohol. He would concede the point and then find something else to grouse about.

As the evening approached, more people came in and, thankfully, it was impossible for Janis to think about anything but filling orders.

At six o'clock Sawyer walked in alone. He greeted several people as he wove his way to a booth in Janis's section. Janis couldn't help the way her heart leaped at the sight of him.

"Sawyer, I don't usually see you in here during the week," she said in greeting.

"I wanted to come in to see how you were doing,"

he replied. He placed his brown cowboy hat next to him on the seat.

"I'm okay," she replied.

"I wanted to call you earlier, but I realized we didn't exchange phone numbers last night. Want to do it now?"

Her heart fluttered. "Sure." She pulled her cell phone from her back pocket, pleased that last night's drama hadn't put him off.

"Can I get you the usual?" she asked once they'd shared their numbers. His usual would be a tall glass of beer.

He hesitated a moment and then shook his head. "No, I think today I'd like just a plain soda with a couple of limes thrown in."

She tried to hide her surprise. "Okay. I'll be right back with it."

Annie met her at the bar. "Oh, my God, Janis. He must be so into you," she said. "He never comes in here by himself or on a weekday."

"I know," Janis replied. But he wouldn't be so into her when she told him the truth about their night of passion. She needed to tell him. It was possible he was just being overly nice to her now because he felt guilty about that night.

But she didn't tell him that evening, or the next when he once again showed up and ordered a soda with lime. Instead, when she was between waiting on people, she stood next to his booth and they continued to get to know each other better.

Wednesday evening when he came in, she knew she couldn't put it off another minute. So far their conversations had been pleasant. They'd talked about the nicer weather and his work around the ranch.

He'd told her that Trisha Cahill, who'd married fellow ranch hand Dusty Crawford, was pregnant and that Dusty was over the moon. In turn, she'd told him that she'd heard rancher Abe Breckinridge and his wife, Donna, were down with the flu and that Janine Willis, who worked at the grocery store, had taken a fall and broken her hip.

They'd talked about nothing in depth and she still had no idea how he'd react when he learned what she had done to him.

Even though she got to know him better the more time she spent with him, she'd like to know him even more. She wanted to know what he dreamed about, what life events had made him into who he was, and what he looked for in the future.

But she feared she'd never get to learn those things once she told him how she'd fooled him. And he had every right to be quite angry with her. What had seemed like a funny idea at the moment didn't feel quite so funny now.

She glanced across the bar to where he was in a booth visiting with Chad Bene who worked on the Swanson ranch. The two men were laughing at something and she wished she was seated next to Sawyer in the booth and having fun.

He glanced in her direction and the look he gave her felt sinfully intimate and warmed her from head to toe. Oh, she didn't want to come clean with him. She didn't want the budding romantic relationship with him to end.

She couldn't completely lose her head. She had to remember that the romance she believed might be building between them was based on her lie.

If tonight went as the other two nights had, Sawyer would stay until about ten or so and then leave to go home. Usually by ten on a weekday the bar became fairly deserted.

Tonight, no matter what was going on in the bar, she was going to have that conversation with him. She absolutely, positively, couldn't put it off any longer.

As the clock quickly wound down to the designated hour, a ribbon of tension twisted around her stomach and pressed tight against her chest.

There were only three people left in the bar. They were all seated in Annie's section when Sawyer reached next to him on the booth seat for his hat, a sure sign that he was preparing to head out. She couldn't let him leave tonight without knowing the truth.

She approached the booth. "You getting ready to leave?"

"It's about that time," he replied. "I know tomorrow is your night off and I was wondering if you'd be interested in eating dinner at the café with me again."

"I'd love to. But, before you leave, there's something I really need to tell you and it might make you renege on your offer." Dread and tension once again pressed tightly in her chest.

He frowned and set his hat back down on the seat. "And what would that be?"

She sucked in a deep breath and then released it.

"We didn't sleep together the other night. I mean, we slept together, but we didn't have sex."

His frown deepened and a dark wariness jumped into his eyes. "What are you talking about? I was there."

"Well, you mostly weren't there," she replied. She stared down at the booth table, unable to meet his gaze as she continued. "You were passed out, like you usually are at the end of a Saturday night. It was kind of a joke, but I also wanted to show you how vulnerable you are when you get in that state. It frightens me for you."

When her words were met with a weighty silence, she finally looked up. Anger. It was written in the darkness of his eyes, in the grim slash of his lips. Every line in his face appeared sharper and his shoulders were stiff.

"Did everyone have a good laugh at my expense?" he asked, the words clipped and curt.

"It wasn't like that," she quickly protested. "I didn't do it for my own humor, although I will admit it was kind of funny seeing your reaction when you woke up in my bed the next morning."

Her words did nothing to soften any of the hardness in his gaze. He leaned over, grabbed his hat once again and worked the brim between his fingers.

"Sawyer, I'll admit something else," she continued hurriedly. "I told you I had a crush on you and I meant it. It's the truth. I didn't like the idea of you being passed out to the point that you could become a victim. You could get beaten up or robbed when you're in that state. You could be taken advantage of by an unscrupulous woman." The words tumbled out of her in a desperate rush to take his anger away.

"So, you decided to be the unscrupulous woman?"

The press of tears burned at her eyes. This was going so much worse than she'd ever thought it would. "I'm sorry. I should have never done it."

"Yeah, you got that right." He got up from the booth, slapped his hat on his head and walked away from her toward the door.

She watched him go until he disappeared from her sight. So much for a romance with Sawyer Quincy. She'd be lucky if he ever spoke to her again.

Sawyer stepped out into the cool night, the air a welcome relief to the hot anger that coursed through him. He wasn't just ticked off at Janis. He was also irritated with his friends, who had obviously been in on the whole thing all along.

Geez, he'd been so worried and had felt so guilty when he'd believed he'd had sex with Janis and had no memory of it. The whole reason he'd invited her out to dinner the next night was that he'd thought they'd been intimate.

But you enjoyed having dinner with her, a small voice whispered in his head. And he'd enjoyed her company since then. Still, he couldn't believe what she had done to him.

He leaned against the front bumper of his truck, let out a deep sigh and stared up the street. Bitterroot shut down early on weeknights and there wasn't a soul on the street except him.

And why was he still there? Why wasn't he already in his truck and driving home?

He had to admit, the whole thing had given him a wake-up call he'd needed for a long time about his drinking. On that same Saturday morning he'd gone to speak to Cassie about the possibility of him becoming foreman once Brody Booth stopped working on the Holiday Ranch.

Brody had found love with Mandy and they now lived on a big spread. Everyone knew he was just biding his time before quitting the Holiday place.

For the first time in his life, Sawyer had wanted to step up and take on additional responsibility, but Cassie had turned him down. She'd said something to the effect that she didn't believe the other men respected him enough to follow his lead.

That night he'd carried a bitter disappointment with him to the bar and he'd tried to drink it away. He'd guzzled his beer down with purpose and, like usual, he hadn't remembered anything after the first couple of beers.

Cassie refusing to consider him for the foreman's job coupled with believing he had made love to a woman while drunk and having no knowledge of it had made him rethink his drinking.

Hell, he didn't even enjoy it that much. Before he could get a nice little buzz going, he always passed out. Was it really possible Janis had a genuine concern about him?

She didn't appear to be the type of woman who would do something like that just for grins and giggles. Maybe she really had done it because she cared about him.

At the moment he was too confused to do anything but head home and get a good night's sleep. He'd figure out how he felt about Janis tomorrow.

He climbed into his truck and instantly spied a piece of paper tucked beneath his windshield wiper.

"What now?" he muttered. He rolled down his window, reached out to grab the paper and then turned on the dome light.

Stay away from her.

Printed in bold, black letters, the words stared up at him. His heart had been racing with anger but it instantly quieted. He looked up and down the street once again, but there was still nobody to see.

As he looked at the note once again, his heart began to beat more quickly. What in the hell? There was no question in his mind that the "her" was Janis.

What was going on? Was this the same work as the person who had spray-painted the back of the bar? If that was the case, he had serious doubts the culprit was Zeke Osmond.

Then who? Did Janis have another boyfriend? Somebody she'd been seeing that Sawyer knew nothing about? Did she maybe have an ex-boyfriend who might be ticked that Sawyer was moving in on what he still thought of as his territory?

The anger he'd felt toward Janis slowly ebbed away. He liked her and he wanted to pursue a relationship with her to see where it led. The note only made him more determined to not stay away from her.

He sat in his truck and thought about everything until it was closing time. Once the bar went dark, he pulled around to the back, got out of his truck and knocked on her door.

She answered immediately, surprise on her features. "Sawyer," she said and opened the door wider to allow him inside.

"We need to talk," he said.

Her gaze searched his face. "I was afraid you'd never want to talk to me again." She motioned him toward the chair. When he was seated, she sank down on the edge of the bed.

"I was definitely angry with you," he admitted.

"I know." She seemed miserable with her shoulders slumped slightly forward and her expressive eyes radiating despair.

"I'll give you the benefit of the doubt that you didn't fool me out of any meanness."

"Oh, Sawyer, being mean to you wasn't ever a thought in my head."

"Then I think it best if we put all that behind us and we start over."

"Really?" Her eyes instantly lightened and relief was evident on her pretty face. "I'd like that a lot."

"And now there's something else I want to talk to you about. Are you seeing somebody else?"

Once again she looked at him in surprise. "Heavens, no."

"Is there an ex-boyfriend lurking around who has been trying to get back together with you?"

"The last boyfriend I had was over two years ago. He didn't even live in Bitterroot and I heard through the grapevine that he got married two months ago. Why are you asking me these questions?"

He stood and pulled the note from his pocket. He unfolded it and handed it to her. "That was under my truck windshield wiper when I left here."

She stared at the note for a long moment and then looked back up at him. "Are you sure this is about me?"

"I'm not seeing anyone else and haven't for a very long time. It's definitely about you."

She dropped the note next to her on the bed as if it burned her fingers. "I can't imagine who would do such a thing."

"I can't, either, but I think we need to call Dillon."

"Do you really think that's necessary?"

He nodded, pulled his cell phone from his back pocket and sat back down in the chair. "I do. This needs to be reported, especially on top of the spray-painting incident that took place. I'll call him."

"Sawyer, I just want to tell you again how very sorry I am," she said when he'd finished making the call.

"I accept your apology and, if truth be known, I should probably thank you," he admitted.

"Thank me?" She looked at him curiously.

He heaved a deep sigh. "Between you and Cassie, my eyes have been opened to my drinking issue."

"Cassie?"

He frowned thoughtfully, remembering his conversation with his boss.

"Last Saturday morning, I decided to talk to her about me possibly taking over the position of foreman when Brody leaves. Since he got hooked up with Mandy Wright, he's been living on that big ranch of hers and we all know he's about ready to quit the Holiday place to ranch on his own."

"So, what did she say?" She leaned closer to him, her gaze soft and her evocative floral scent swirling around his head.

"She basically said she didn't think I had the respect of the other men because of the nights they have to put me to bed drunk, although she didn't say in it those exact words."

"Why do you drink?"

"I always thought that's just what we did. We worked hard during the week and then went to the bar to drink on Saturday nights," he replied.

"Do you like the taste of beer?"

He frowned thoughtfully. He'd never really considered the things she was asking him about before. "It's all right," he replied.

"I think you're allergic to it or something."

He looked at her in surprise. "You think?"

"I've never seen anyone totally pass out on so few drinks as you do."

"According to my mother, my father was a raging alcoholic who suffered blackouts. I've had a few blackouts, as well."

"You didn't know your father?"

"He disappeared from our life when I was four years old. When I was ten, we heard that he'd died. It's a good guess that he died from his alcoholism."

"My father died from a massive heart attack when I was sixteen." A deep sadness filled her eyes.

"I'm sorry for your loss," he replied. "It stinks not to have a father."

"At least I had mine for sixteen years. You didn't have yours for long at all. Do you have any memories of him?"

"None," he replied.

Before they could talk any further, Dillon arrived. He looked at the note and then asked Janis the same questions Sawyer had asked her. Was she seeing anyone else? Was there somebody she knew who wanted to date her? Maybe somebody she'd turned down recently? Janis's answers were the same…no, no and no.

"It definitely looks to me like you've picked yourself up a secret admirer," Dillon said. "And he might possibly want Sawyer out of the picture so he can make a play for you."

"So, what should we do?" Janis asked.

"I don't think you have anything to worry about," Dillon said to her. "I imagine whoever it is will either make himself known to you pretty quickly or he'll just give up and go away."

He then looked at Sawyer. "I also really don't think you have anything to worry about, either. In my experience, anonymous notes rarely lead to any kind of violent actions."

Sawyer nodded, but that didn't mean he wasn't

going to watch his own back a little more closely than usual. "I'll take the note with me, but I imagine the only prints I'll get will be from the two of you," Dillon continued as he stepped to the door. "There isn't much more I can do at this point."

"Thanks for coming out," Janis said.

"That's my job," the lawman replied with a smile. "I'll let you both know if I manage to pull off any viable prints, but don't hold your breath."

"I should probably get out of here, too," Sawyer said when Dillon had gone. "You still up for dinner at the café with me tomorrow night?"

"Are we okay?" Her eyes held a soft luminosity and her lips had never looked so darned kissable. He pulled her into his arms and settled his mouth over hers.

He kept the kiss light and quick, but it wasn't because her lips didn't entice him to delve deeper. It wasn't because she didn't excite him on a physical level.

It was because he really did want to take things slow with her. He wanted a do-over. Things had gotten off to such a crazy start with them and now that he knew he hadn't made love to her, he was excited for them to slowly progress to that place.

"So, how about I pick you up around five thirty tomorrow?" he said when the kiss ended.

"I'll be ready and waiting," she replied. "I work

the morning shift and get off at three thirty, so that gives me plenty of time to clean up."

Minutes later, when he was back in his truck and headed home, he thought again about the note. Was it simply from some timid soul who had a crush on Janis or was it the beginning of something more ominous?

He figured if he wound up dead, it would either be from Halena Redwing pinching his butt to death or because they all should have taken the note more seriously.

Only time would tell, and that thought did nothing to make him feel better.

Chapter 4

"I've looked forward to this all day," Janis said to Sawyer as they entered the busy café the next evening.

"Ah, you're just here because they have great french fries," he replied, his eyes filled with a teasing light.

"There is that," she agreed. She was thrilled that he didn't seem to harbor any bad feelings toward her. She definitely liked a man who forgave easily.

They spied an empty booth and wove their way through the tables toward it. Once they were seated, he gazed at her seriously. "How are you doing after last night?"

"Better now," she replied. "But I'll admit I had

a hard time getting to sleep. I keep thinking about all the men I have contact with at the bar and who might have written that note to you."

"Did you come up with any answers?"

"Unfortunately no. There are lots of men who are flirtatious with me, but it's all harmless fun."

She didn't want to tell him that last night, for the first time since she'd moved into the room in the back of the bar, she'd felt a bit creeped out. Was her secret admirer parked someplace nearby watching her door? After Sawyer had left, had her admirer crept up to her window to peer inside? Those were the kinds of disturbing thoughts that had kept sleep at bay.

As ridiculous as it was, she'd felt eyes watching her, raising the hair on the nape of her neck and making it hard for her to breathe.

"I don't want to talk about that tonight," she finally said. "I just want to talk about happy things."

He smiled at her. "So, what kinds of things make you happy?"

"A rainstorm while I sleep and sheets that smell like sunshine," she said thoughtfully. "Chocolate ice cream, and thinking about someday having my own house, and a wiggly little puppy make me happy. What about you?"

He leaned back. "I never really thought about it much before, but listening to Mac strum his guitar and riding across the pasture on my horse makes me happy. Do you ride?"

"No, I've never even been on a horse," she replied.

"Well, we're definitely going to have to change that." Anything else he was going to say was interrupted by Julia Hatfield arriving to take their orders.

For the next twenty minutes they talked about the new menu items Mandy had added since taking over the café and what kinds of food they liked and what they didn't like.

Tonight Sawyer had ordered a fried-chicken dinner complete with a mound of mashed potatoes and corn. Janis had opted for one of the new items: a turkey and avocado wrap with fries on the side.

As they ate, he entertained her with more stories about the men he not only worked with but had also grown up with, and of Big Cass who had taken a chance on them all.

"She had a soft side, but she could also be as tough as nails. None of us ever wanted to disappoint her. She gave us all respect when most of us had never had it and she taught us to respect ourselves."

"I saw her around town once in a while, but I never met her," Janis replied.

He shook his head and smiled, a soft light in his eyes. "She was something else. It's hard to believe she's been gone for almost a year now. She definitely filled a hole inside me that my mother's death had left behind."

"You and your mother were close?"

"Very," he replied. "It was always just her and me against the world. She was beautiful and loving, and pretty much the center of my world. I never doubted how much she loved me."

"That's nice," Janis said wistfully. "I felt that way about my father. I was his princess and he made me feel like the most loved person in the world."

"But you aren't close to your mother," Sawyer said.

"No, I'm not. Tell me more about your mother," she said in an attempt to deflect the conversation away from her relationship with her mother.

She'd never shared with anyone the fact that her mother had never loved her. That her father's unconditional and enormous love had never been quite enough to fill the void in Janis's heart that her mother's hatred of her had left behind.

As they lingered over coffee, Sawyer told her about growing up poor and with a mother who struggled to keep a roof over their heads and food on the table. "We ate ketchup spaghetti and lots of potatoes, and considered it a treat if she managed to buy any kind of meat."

"Didn't she qualify for some sort of assistance?" Janis asked.

"I'm sure she did, but she didn't believe in the government taking care of us. She said as long as she was able-bodied and could work, we'd get by," he said.

"What kind of work did she do?"

"She cleaned houses. She said it was the best job for her because she could manage her hours so she was always there for me when I got out of school." Sawyer's voice was filled with his love for the woman who had given him birth.

"And what kind of a kid were you? Were you good and dutiful or were you ornery?"

"Maybe a little bit of both," he admitted with a laugh. "I definitely had my share of ornery."

She smiled at him. It was so easy to envision him as a red-haired little boy with a naughty grin on his face and mischief in his eyes.

She was sorry when their coffee was gone and the night had reached its logical conclusion. It was time for him to take her home.

The night air felt almost balmy compared to what it had been. "Oh, I hope this means spring has really arrived," she said once she was in the passenger seat.

"All the men at the ranch can't wait for nicer days. We've all been cooped up together for too long during the winter."

"Clay certainly doesn't seem to let winter slow him down when it comes to dating," she said. Clay Madison had a reputation for being the town's Romeo.

He laughed and shook his head as he started the truck. "That boy is something else. I think he's dated almost all the single women in the state of Oklahoma, and the surprising thing is, they all continue to love him even when he breaks up with them."

She laughed. "He definitely comes across as a charmer with more than a bit of mischief."

"That he is," Sawyer replied. He started to back out of the parking space but there was a clunk that halted him. "What the heck?" He threw the truck back into Park. "Sit tight. That feels like a flat tire."

He got out of the truck and walked around. When he got to her side, he threw up his arms and scowled.

She rolled down her window.

"Do you want the bad news first or the bad news last?" he asked.

"The tire is flat?" she asked.

He nodded. "As a pancake, and I don't have a spare. I loaned it to Flint and I haven't gotten it back from him yet. I need to call Larry Wright to see if he can hook me up with a tire."

Janis knew Larry Wright owned the only car lot in town and that his business also did repairs.

At that moment, Gary pulled into the parking space next to them and peered out his window. "Uh, oh. Somebody has a problem." Gary was with his eldest daughter, Kayla.

"Yeah. I don't have a spare, so I'm about to call Larry to see if he can hook me up," Sawyer replied.

"Kayla and I are here to have a little father-daughter bonding time over dessert, but, Janis, if you need a ride home, we can take you there," Gary replied.

"Oh, no, I'll just wait for Sawyer," she said.

"No, you won't," Sawyer said firmly and opened her truck door. "I have no idea how long I'll be." He turned back to look at Gary. "I really appreciate it, Gary. There's no sense in her sitting here cooling her heels for what might take hours."

"No problem," Gary replied. "Come on, Janis. It will just take a few minutes and then Kayla and I can come back and get our dessert."

Minutes later, Janis was in the seat behind Kayla in the van. "I haven't seen you in a while, Kayla. How's life treating you?" Janis had known both of Gary's girls for years.

The pretty, dark-haired girl turned in the seat to smile at Janis. "Not too bad. Did you hear I got my veterinarian license and I'm now working with Dan Richards?" Dan Richards had been Bitterroot's only vet for years.

"I did hear that," Janis replied. "Your daddy has been crowing with pride at your success."

Gary crowed like a rooster, making the two women laugh. They pulled up behind the bar and Janis retrieved her key from her purse.

"Thanks for the ride, Gary. I really appreciate it," she said as she stepped out of the van. "Enjoy the father-daughter time."

"We always do," Gary replied.

He waited to pull away until she'd unlocked the door and stepped inside. She then waved to them and closed and relocked the door.

She flopped down on the bed and released a deep sigh, disappointed by how the night had ended. She enjoyed Sawyer's company so much. Not only did he excite her but she also felt completely comfortable in his presence.

She wasn't fool enough to believe they were in love. In fact, Janis had never been in love. Although the one man she'd had a fairly serious relationship with in the past had professed to be in love with her, she'd ultimately broken up with him.

She pulled herself up off the bed and changed from her clothes into a light blue cotton nightshirt that had a cute, snoozing unicorn on the front.

The sexy nightgown she'd worn for the night with Sawyer had been bought long ago for show and not for a comfortable night's sleep. She much preferred cotton to silk when it came to nightwear.

Although it was relatively early, she got into bed and grabbed a notebook from the nightstand drawer. On the front was a label that read My House.

It was her dream book and sometimes on her day off she spent hours thumbing through magazines and cutting out pictures of furniture and floor plans, of bedspreads and curtains and lawn decorations.

The vision of her owning a home had been created in the year she had been virtually homeless. On those nights when she found herself sleeping in her car, or on a sofa in a friend's place, she longed for a place to call her very own, a place where nobody could kick her out or grow tired of her.

It was strange… In all her dreams of her future and having a house of her own, she'd never imagined a man there. She'd dreamed about sitting at her kitchen table to enjoy a morning cup of coffee, of planting a small garden in the backyard, and of sitting on a back deck to watch the sun go down. But in all those dreams, she was always alone.

Although she liked Sawyer, it was a little too early to adjust her dreams to include him.

She scarcely paid attention to the noise coming from the bar. Long ago she'd gotten used to the music and laughter that filled her room whenever the bar was open and she was off work.

She had no idea how much time had passed with her lost in dreams about what kind of home she'd hopefully own one day when a knock fell on her door.

Suddenly thinking about her secret admirer, a chill washed over her. She got out of bed and padded to the door, wondering if she should open it or not.

Another knock sounded. "Janis, are you there? It's me."

Relief, along with a little surprise, winged through her at the sound of Sawyer's deep voice.

She opened the door and motioned him inside. "What are you doing here?" she asked.

"A gentleman always sees that his date gets home safely," he replied.

Warmth swept into her heart. "I'm assuming your truck is now sporting a new tire?"

"Yeah. I'm taking it in tomorrow to get another new one on the other side. But I don't want to talk about that. It's obvious you're ready for bed and I don't want to keep you. I just thought we needed to end the date on a more appropriate note."

"An appropriate note?"

He reached out and pulled her into his arms. He lowered his mouth to hers. His lips plied hers with a heat that usurped any chill she might have felt when he had first knocked on the door.

His tongue touched hers, as if tentatively requesting entry. She opened her mouth wider to allow the deeper kiss. Oh, and what a kiss it was.

Their tongues swirled together and she leaned closer into him. His arms tightened around her and he pulled her closer...closer still, until she was flush against him, breast against chest and hips against hips.

His heart beat fast against hers...or was it her own that banged so quickly? A thrill fluttered through her as she realized he was aroused.

Before she could really process that fact, he dropped his arms to his sides and stepped back from her. "Oh, woman," he murmured and then raked a hand through his hair. His eyes torched a glazed heat as he stared at her.

At that moment, if he'd wanted to take her to bed, she would have gone willingly. Instead he broke eye contact and opened the door, as if needing the night air to cool the unexpected fire that had flamed to life with their kiss.

When he gazed at her again, the fire in his eyes was gone but the smile he offered her was a sensual, intimate gesture that warmed her from the top of her head to the very tip of her toes.

"If this nice weather holds, how would you like to come out to the ranch on Sunday for a little fishing and a picnic?"

"That sounds heavenly," she replied.

He backed out the door. "Then why don't we plan for me to pick you up around one?"

"Sounds good to me."

Good-nights were said and then he was gone.

Minutes later Janis sat on the side of her bed, her head filled with thoughts of him. She touched her lips thoughtfully, the memory of his still burning hers with heat. There was no question that they shared a wild, physical chemistry. She was just happy that apparently he felt it as strongly as she did.

She shivered with remembered pleasure as she replayed their kiss in her mind. She had a feeling she would never get tired of his kisses.

In two days she would spend time alone with him again. She couldn't wait. It had been a long time since she'd felt this sweet anticipation, this wild yearning to be with a man. She prayed that the weather remained good for Sunday.

She was ready to get into bed when an eeriness struck her. It was the kind of eeriness that raised the hairs on the nape of her neck and shot goose bumps up and down her arms.

Was somebody watching her right now? Standing just outside her window and peeking in through the crack in the curtains? A new chill suffused her body.

That was what it felt like…like somebody was watching her. She stared at the nearby window but remained frozen in place for several long moments.

Just look out the window, a small voice niggled in her mind. There was no way she'd go to sleep unless she checked it out. She had to see if somebody was there. She drew in a deep, shuddery breath, raced to the window and threw open the curtains.

Nobody.

She whooshed out a breath of relief. Not only was there nobody around her window, there wasn't a vehicle parked anywhere nearby except her own.

Her imagination had to be working overtime. She pulled the curtains tightly closed and then got into bed. Still, it was a very long time before she finally fell asleep.

When Sawyer got back to the ranch, instead of going into his room, he rounded the building and entered the dining and rec area. He was pleased to find several of the other cowboys still up.

Mac McBride sat in one of the recliners, his guitar next to him. Flint McCay and Jerod Steen shared one of the sofas and Clay sat in another recliner.

They all greeted him as he sank down on one end of another sofa. "You just missed Mac's music," Clay said. "He's been strumming and singing for us for the last half an hour."

"I'm just glad to find some of you still awake," Sawyer replied.

"What's up?" Flint asked. "You look a bit troubled."

"I am a little bit troubled," Sawyer confessed. "I took Janis out to dinner tonight and when we came out of the café to head home, I had a flat tire."

"Uh, oh," Flint said with a wince. "I just remembered I owe you a tire."

"I'm not worried about that. What does have me a little worried is that the tire was intentionally flattened. It had a deep slash in it that could have only happened with a big, sharp knife."

He told them about the note he'd found, but didn't mention the spray painting. He kept that to himself out of respect for Janis. He hadn't told Janis that the tire had been intentionally flattened because he hadn't wanted to worry her.

"And you don't have any idea who might be responsible?" Clay asked.

Sawyer shook his head. "Not a clue. And the only thing I can think of is that somebody wants to make it as hard as possible on me to date Janis."

"Have you considered not dating her anymore?" Mac asked.

"No, that's not going to happen," he replied. He liked the way her smiles warmed his heart. He enjoyed their conversations and kissing her had set him on fire. No, there was no way he intended to stop seeing her. She might or might not be the woman he'd been waiting for. She could be the woman he wanted to marry and build a family with, but he'd never know if she was that woman if he stopped seeing her now.

"So, what do you need from us?" Clay asked.

"Watch my back?"

"You know it," Flint replied.

"I'm not too worried at the moment," Sawyer continued. "An anonymous note and a flat tire doesn't exactly have me shivering in my boots."

"Still, you're smart to watch your back," Mac replied. "And on that note, I'm headed off to bed." He grabbed his guitar and stood.

Flint got up, as well. "Me, too. Sunrise is coming earlier and earlier these days."

Jerod joined them and minutes later Sawyer and Clay were left alone. "Janis doesn't know who this creep might be?" Clay asked.

"She says she can't imagine who it might be."

"It's got to be somebody who hangs out at the bar."

Sawyer nodded in agreement. "Yeah. I plan to hang out at the bar after work each day to see if I can figure out who he might be. You ever been through something like this?"

"No, nothing like this."

"I just figured with all the women you bed, you might have run across some jealous man who wanted to beat your hide."

Clay laughed. "Let me let you in on a little secret, my friend. I'm not, and I haven't been, sleeping with most of the women I date. My reputation is definitely way overblown." His smile faded. "I'm just looking for that right one. You know, the woman I want to wake up with every morning for the rest of my life. I'm looking for my life partner. Unfortunately, I haven't found her yet."

"I don't know if Janis is the woman I want to be with for the rest of my life, but I'll be damned if I let some anonymous creep try to keep me away from her," Sawyer said firmly.

"You'd better just hope that creep doesn't find you on a Saturday night when the rest of us aren't around," Clay said. "He could beat the hell out of you and you wouldn't be the wiser until you sobered up."

"I'm not drinking anymore."

Clay looked at him in surprise. "For real?"

"For real. I've decided I'm way too old to need

babysitters after having a few beers. Besides, I've never really enjoyed drinking."

"Does this mean you won't be coming to the Watering Hole with us on Saturday nights anymore?" Clay asked.

"I'll still go out with you all, I just won't be drinking anything alcoholic anymore. Besides, as long as I'm seeing Janis, I imagine I'll be spending a lot more time at the Watering Hole. Just think, if I do go out with you all, you won't have to carry me home and put me to bed. And I won't have to worry about waking up in the mornings with strange things in my bed. I think I'll enjoy my Saturday nights and Sunday mornings even more if I'm sober."

Clay grinned. "You know you will be taking away some of our fun. We worked hard at being creative when it came to putting things in your bed."

"So now you'll have to find another outlet for your creativity."

"Sounds good to me, brother. And on that note, I'm heading to bed," Clay said as he stood. "You'll let us know if anything else happens that you see as a threat."

"Trust me, you all will be the first to know." Sawyer pulled himself out of the chair and together the two men left the rec room and headed to the front of the building. "Good night, Clay," Sawyer said as he stopped at his bunk room door.

"'Night, Sawyer. See you in the morning."

* * *

The next evening Sawyer ate dinner with the rest of the men in the cowboy dining room and then showered and headed into town.

Clay was probably right. Whoever Janis's secret admirer might be probably spent a lot of time in the bar. Did he sit in a corner and watch her? Dreaming about the two of them being together?

The idea made Sawyer sick. If the man was so into Janis then why hadn't he asked her out? Why was he hiding in the shadows with his desire for her?

And certainly he must entertain some sort of desire for her, otherwise what was the purpose of the note? Why slash his tire if not in an attempt to somehow complicate things and make Sawyer stay away from her?

These were the dark thoughts swirling around in his head as he walked into the Watering Hole. However the darkness lifted momentarily when he saw Janis.

She was working behind the bar tonight. As she saw him, her features lit up and the smile she shot him warmed him. It was funny, before the night they'd spent together, he'd found her smiles attractive, but they hadn't quickened his heartbeat as they did now.

He swept his hat off his head, ambled over to the bar and sat on one of the empty stools.

Immediately she was standing in front of him.

"Hi, cowboy," she said, her beautiful eyes sparkling brightly. "What can I get a man to parch his thirst after riding the range all day?"

"The usual," he replied. "But with an extra twist of lime."

"Coming right up." She moved down the length of the bar and, as she did, he turned on the stool to check out who was there on a Friday night.

It was still relatively early in the evening for the usual crowd to be in the bar. But before the night was over, the place would be rocking with people and noise.

Nobody at the tables or booths appeared to be paying any special attention to the bar or specifically to Janis. Yet he was convinced that the person who harbored a secret thing for her was a regular patron.

"Here we are." Janis's voice turned him back around on the stool.

"Thank you, ma'am." He grinned at her. "And might I add that you're the prettiest thing in this entire place." He was surprised to see her face color with a charming blush.

"Thank you, and might I add that you're the most handsome cowboy I've seen all night."

Once again he smiled at her. "Okay, enough of that. How are you doing?"

"Good. I'm praying that this great weather holds so we can go fishing on Sunday."

"Are you a good fisherman or one of those women who squeals at the sight of a wiggling worm?"

She laughed. "I don't know whether I'll catch any fish or not, but I can bait my own hook without squealing. It's been years since I've fished. My dad used to take me before he died."

"I have a feeling we're going to have a great day," he replied. He was with her now, but he already couldn't wait until the next time he saw her. It had been a very long time since he'd felt this way about a woman.

"I absolutely, positively, know we're going to have a great day," she replied.

"Hey, Janis," Myles Hennessy called from the other end of the bar. "Darlin', I need another one." He held up an empty glass.

"Duty calls," she said and then hurried down the length of the bar to serve Myles.

Sawyer leaned against the back of the stool and took a sip of the lime-flavored soda. Would he walk out of here tonight and discover another flat tire? Or maybe a shattered window? How he wished he knew who was behind it.

Once again he swiveled around to check out the growing crowd of people. He frowned as a group of Humes's men walked in, including Zeke. Thank goodness Janis was working behind the bar and wouldn't have to deal with any of them tonight.

Again, he didn't see anyone who appeared to be

watching Janis. He turned around once again and swept his gaze across the people seated on the stools.

The men who chose to sit at the bar were usually the single men of Bitterroot. They were the loners and the lonely, the disenfranchised and the men who took their drinking seriously.

Next to Myles was Damon West, a widower who had lost his wife to breast cancer three years ago. Was it possible he was looking for a new wife and had chosen Janis to fill that role?

Seated at the other end of the bar was John Bailey, a forty-something man who had never been married. Did he harbor a secret thing for Janis? Hell, it could be anybody she served a drink to.

Too many suspects and not enough information, he thought with frustration. So far everything that had happened had been pretty benign. What concerned him was the possibility that things would escalate. And if that happened, he hoped nobody got hurt... or killed.

Chapter 5

Bright sunshine greeted Janis on Sunday morning when she woke up, and the sight of it filled her heart with happy anticipation. This afternoon she would once again have Sawyer all to herself.

He'd come in last night with his Holiday Ranch tribe and she'd been happy when he'd ordered soda instead of beer. He appeared to be all-in on the no drinking policy and she was so pleased that he'd made that decision for himself.

Whether she was together with him or not in the future, he'd be a better man in staying away from alcohol. But today she didn't even want to think about him not being in her future. She intended to just enjoy each and every minute she shared with him.

By twelve forty-five she was clad in a pair of jeans, a light blue T-shirt, and had a navy sweater in her hands as she stood at her door waiting for him to arrive.

Would she always feel this kind of crazy anticipation when she knew she was going to see him, to be with him again? She hoped so, but she also knew there was still a lot to learn about each other. It was possible that ultimately they would discover things about each other that would make them realize they had no future together.

She'd never really believed she'd ever find a man who would want to spend the rest of his life with her. All her plans, all her dreams for the future, had been built on the notion that she would be alone.

But as Sawyer's truck pulled in, she had a moment of hoping that maybe her dreams really could be revised to include a special cowboy.

You'll never find a man who really loves you because you're nothing but a dirty little whore. The strident voice echoed loudly in her head.

"No," she whispered aloud. She shoved the hateful voice, and the pain it always brought with it, away as she left her room and hurried to the truck. She absolutely, positively, refused to allow any negative thoughts to screw up her day with Sawyer.

He greeted her with one of his sexy smiles as she slid into the passenger seat. "You ready for a fishing contest?"

"What do I get if I win?"

"Ha, that's a real optimistic question. Maybe you should ask what the loser gets," he replied.

She shot him a cheeky grin. "Maybe I don't care what you're going to get as the loser."

He laughed and that set the mood for the day.

They reached the Holiday Ranch and she sobered as he told her about the shed that was going to be built over the burial site of the seven teenagers Adam Benson, the former foreman of the ranch, had killed.

When the spring tornado had ripped across the land, it had not only taken Big Cass's life but the cleanup had unearthed the seven skeletons. It had not only been an unsettling discovery for all the men who lived there, but also for the entire town of Bitterroot.

She sat up taller with interest as he drove across the greening pasture and to the pond that sparkled in the afternoon sunshine.

"I've got a big picnic basket packed full of goodies, but I thought maybe we'd fish for a little while before eating," he said as he shut off the truck engine.

"Sounds good to me," she replied.

Minutes later they sat on the end of the small dock that extended out over the pond, their poles dangling over the water. "Do you always wear a gun when you go fishing?" she asked, noting the weapon in the holster on his hip.

"Whenever we're out in the pasture, we all usually wear our guns. You never know when you might encounter a wild critter."

"What kind of wild critters?" she asked.

"There are snakes and an occasional coyote, but we're always on the lookout for the abominable thingamagoblin."

"The thingamagoblin? Oo-oh, that sounds really scary," she replied, loving the twinkle that lit his eyes.

"It is a terrible thing to behold. None of us has really gotten close to one, but it's said to be a big, hairy beast who has big fangs for teeth. It's large enough to carry a full-grown cow and it makes a kind of squealing cry that chills a man to his very bones."

"Then I'm glad I have a big, strong cowboy to protect me from such a beast," she said with a mock shiver.

"My pleasure, ma'am." Together they laughed. "You told me the other night that your dad used to take you fishing. Tell me about him."

Memories filled her head, happy memories tinged with a pang of sorrow.

"As far as I'm concerned, he was the best father a child could have ever had. When I was small, each morning I would curl up in his lap at the breakfast table and he'd hold me for a few minutes before my day began. When I started school, he always had something special planned afterward for us to do together before dinner. Not only did he teach me to fish and how to shoot a gun, but he also took me shopping for pretty dresses and to the beauty shop to get my hair and nails done."

Oh, she couldn't begin to tell him everything that had made her childhood with her father so magical. He was the man who had taught her not only how to respect nature but also how to dance. He'd understood her life-or-death need to have a backpack covered in bright red hearts in the fifth grade, and he'd consoled her that same year when mean girl Dana Witherspoon had told her she'd never be popular because she was too stupid and plain.

"What did he do for a living?" Sawyer asked, pulling her from her inner thoughts.

"He worked at the bank as a loan officer. He once told me that his greatest joy was when he could loan people the money they needed and one of his greatest sorrows was when he had to tell somebody no."

Sawyer took his hat off and raked his fingers through his hair. He eyed her with a twinkle of humor. "So, were you a good kid or were you a little bit ornery?"

"Definitely a good kid." Her fingers itched to reach out and stroke through his hair that sparkled so enchantingly in the sunshine.

"I was an excellent student and I toed the line. Not because I was afraid of punishment, but because I never wanted to be a disappointment to my parents, especially my father."

Her line jerked. "Oh, I think I've got a bite." She scrambled to her feet.

Sawyer quickly joined her. "Don't lose it."

She jerked the line and began to reel in. "I've got it," she exclaimed with excitement. She kept tension on the line and a few moments later pulled in the smallest little catfish she'd ever seen.

Sawyer laughed. "The way you were reeling, I thought you were going to pull in a whale. That little fish doesn't hardly count as a catch."

"Ha, but in the contest of who is going to catch the biggest fish, right now I'm in first place," she replied.

He laughed again. "I'll give you that, but our fishing time isn't over yet."

They fished for another hour or so, but no more fish were caught. "Looks like I'm the big winner of the day," she said as they reeled up their poles in preparation of enjoying their picnic. "And you never told me what the prize was for the winner."

He took her pole from her hand and then placed them in the rear of his pickup. He turned back to her and his eyes were lit with a shine that half stole her breath away.

"The prize is a kiss," he said, drawing her into his arms. He then planted a kiss on her forehead and released her.

She stood still, disappointed in her prize. Why had he kissed her on the forehead? Had he found her kisses wanting in some way? He certainly hadn't acted like it the last time he'd kissed her.

He grabbed a large cooler basket from the back and gazed at her again. "You ready to eat?"

"Yes, but what I really want to know right now is why you didn't kiss me on the lips."

His eyes once again flamed with heat. "Oh, woman, I have to pick and choose when I kiss you on the lips because kissing you is way too hot and exciting. If I kiss you right now, then I might not want to stop, and you deserve far better than a roll in the grass in a pasture."

A warm thrill sizzled through her at his words. Sawyer Quincy was definitely working his way quickly into her heart. "Okay, now I'm ready to eat," she said.

He maneuvered the picnic basket onto one shoulder and then grabbed her hand as they walked to an area near the pond. A happiness she'd never known before filled her. It made the budding green leaves on the trees look brighter and the smell of early spring flowers much sharper. The sky appeared more blue than ever before and the birds all sang happy melodies.

They reached a lovely spot with mature trees surrounding a large clearing. He opened the basket and pulled out a big red-and-white-checkered tablecloth. "Get comfortable and prepare for a feast," he said.

As she sat on one corner of the tablecloth, he

began pulling out cold drinks and then container after container. "My goodness, you weren't kidding about a feast," she said. "Did you pack all this?"

He knelt on his knees to finish unloading. "If I was smart, I'd tell you I spent all morning putting this food together especially for us."

"And if you weren't smart?" she asked.

He grinned at her. "I'd have to confess and tell you that the truth is I had nothing to do with the food. Last night I told Cookie that I was having a picnic with a special lady today and he did the rest. Why don't you start opening the containers and let's see what we have."

By the time he sat, she'd revealed ham-and-cheese sandwiches, potato salad and a medley of bite-size fruit. There was also potato chips, bread and butter pickles, and brownies for dessert.

"Unfortunately there are no french fries, but maybe one night you can eat dinner with us men on the ranch and get a taste of Cookie's seasoned fries."

"I'd like that," she replied, pleased that he wouldn't mind her being around his friends when she wasn't serving them at the bar. "It's so nice out here. It's a good place to listen to nature's heartbeat, as my father used to say."

"I think I would have liked your father," he said. They began to fill the sturdy paper plates Cookie had provided.

While they ate, they talked about the food, the

birds in the trees and the fish they'd caught in the past. She believed most of his stories, but when he told her that he'd once pulled in a crappie almost as big as his horse, she cried foul.

When the leftovers were packed in the basket, they stretched out side-by-side on their backs. She looked up at the blue of the sky and released a deep sigh of satisfaction.

They were silent, but it was a comfortable quiet. The scent of his cologne eddied in the air and filled her with both a simmering desire and a sense of contentment.

"I'm glad you aren't a woman who feels the need to fill every silence with a lot of chatter," he said after a few minutes.

She rolled over onto her side and propped herself up on one elbow. "I've always been comfortable with silence. I spend a lot of time alone, so the silence is familiar to me."

"Did you always plan to be a bartender?" He changed his positon to mirror hers.

"Heavens, no," she replied with a laugh. She sobered as she remembered what had once been some of her dreams for her future. "My dad wanted me to go to college and get a degree in accounting or maybe nursing. 'Money-people and health-care workers will always have a job,' he used to tell me."

"So why didn't that happen?" Sawyer asked.

She shrugged. "Things changed when dad died.

My mother told me there wasn't money for college. By the time I turned eighteen, all I wanted was to get out on my own. I had my car and a handful of plans that had nothing to do with real life."

"I think I know about all those plans," he said. "I imagine they were the same ones I had when I left home."

She nodded. "I figured it would be easy to be out on my own. I'd get a great job and an awesome apartment. I'd work hard and build a wonderful future for myself."

She'd show her mother. That's what had driven her out of her house and out on her own the day she'd graduated from high school. She'd do great things and make her mother regret all the hateful, hurtful, things she'd ever said to Janis.

"So, what did you do?" he asked. His gaze searched her features, as if trying to memorize them.

The sun was warm, but his gaze made her warmer and suddenly she didn't want to talk about her past anymore. She wanted to see his beautiful eyes light with humor. She wanted to hear the sound of his deep laughter.

"Thankfully, Gary gave me a job when I turned nineteen, along with the room to live in. The bottom line is I survived and now here I am with you, as the official winner of a fishing contest."

Sure enough, his eyes twinkled and a sexy smile

slid across his lips. "How long do you intend to keep crowing about this fishing thing?"

"Until we fish together again and you figure out how to beat me," she replied.

"Maybe we should fish a little more right now," he replied.

She grinned. "You're just eager to take away my championship status."

"I am. But before we get to the fishing, there's something I want to do."

"What's that?"

He leaned forward and captured her lips with his. Sweet fire swept through her and her heart quickened its pace. Her impulse was to lean forward, to get closer to him. But he made no move toward her and, before she knew it, he'd ended the kiss.

Instead he abruptly got to his feet. "Come on, woman. Let's see if I can catch a fish bigger than your little minnow." He held out a hand to her.

Although she would have lain on the tablecloth and kissed Sawyer forever, she grabbed his hand and allowed him to help her to her feet for more fishing adventure.

Instantly, a loud pop resounded, sending birds to fly from the treetops. "Get down," Sawyer yelled at her.

What was happening? Before her mind could make sense of things, Sawyer threw her to the ground and covered her body with his. All of his muscles were tensed and her heart fluttered with fear as he pulled his gun and pointed it toward a nearby stand of trees.

Another pop smashed the silence and Sawyer returned fire despite the fact that he could see no target. Whoever it was had the cover of trees while he and Janis were out in the open like two sitting ducks.

His brain worked overtime to digest the fact that somebody was shooting at them. But his number-one priority was to get Janis to safety.

His truck wasn't parked too far away. At least that would provide her with some kind of cover. All he had to do was to get her out from beneath him and to the vehicle.

He had no idea who the shooter was trying to hit, but what he did know was those two bullets had whizzed precariously close to his head.

"Janis, I need you to run to the truck," he said softly. Her body tensed beneath his. He thought he could feel the frantic beat of her heart but, under the circumstances, it was hard to tell if it was hers or his own doing the quick thudding. At least she wasn't screaming like a banshee as many might do under the circumstances.

"Okay." Her reply was a mere warm whisper against his neck.

"On the count of three, I'm going to roll off you

and start shooting. You run like hell to the truck and get on the other side of it. You should be safe there."

"But…but what about you?" she asked with a touch of frantic fear.

"I'll be all right," he lied. In truth, he had no idea if he'd get out of this situation alive or not. He hoped like hell he would, otherwise he worried about what would happen to Janis if he wound up dead and his killer went after her.

"One…" He felt her body tense even more. "Two…" Her gasp heated his throat. "Three." He rolled off her and at the same time fired several shots toward the general area where he knew the shooter was hiding.

He was grateful that no shots stymied Janis from reaching the safety and the cover of the truck. She had been a relatively easy target as she'd run away, but Sawyer had the idea that the person with the gun wanted him dead, not her.

The next gunshots proved that point. The bullets were directed at Sawyer, whizzing by him first on the left side and then on the right.

Sooner or later the bastard was going to get lucky and hit his mark. Sawyer rolled once again. At least he could make it more difficult by keeping on the move.

It was possible he could roll enough to reach the tree line and there he would have some much-needed cover. He rolled again. Another shot fired.

Dust kicked up so close to him he tasted it in the back of his throat, along with a healthy dose of fear.

He was afraid to get up into a crouch and make himself a bigger target. He continued to move, slithering like a snake against the ground to get to the trees.

The thunder of horses' hooves sounded from the distance and jetted a wave of relief through Sawyer. At the same time a gunshot sounded again and a searing pressure ripped through the top of his shoulder. Crap, he'd been hit. Burning pain fired through him, making him feel half nauseous.

He'd never been so happy to see Clay, Mac and Flint, all riding hell-bent for leather toward him. "Over there," he said and pointed to the woods. "A shooter."

They all dismounted, guns drawn. Mac and Flint ran for the woods and Clay hurried to Sawyer's side. "Oh, man, you've been hit," he exclaimed. "How bad is it?"

"I'm okay," Sawyer said as he sat up. The nausea had passed, leaving only a white-hot, searing pain behind. "Go check on Janis, she's somewhere by the truck."

As Clay ran toward the truck, Sawyer got to his feet and pressed a hand against his burning, bleeding wound. He wasn't worried about the man in the woods taking another shot at him, not with Mac and

Flint hunting him down. He'd be too busy turning tail and escaping to take any more shots.

What he was most concerned about was Janis. She had to be terrified by the horrible turn the afternoon had taken. He raced to the truck and found her seated on the ground next to the back tire with Clay standing next to her.

"Sawyer!" She got to her feet, her face pale and her eyes huge. Her eyes grew even wider as she saw the blood on his shirt. "Oh, my God, you're hurt!"

"I'll be all right. Let's get you out of here," he replied. "Clay, you want to drive her back to the big house and have Cassie call Dillon, if he isn't there. I'll take your horse back."

"Sawyer, he was shooting at you," Janis protested. "You can't ride a horse back to the house. You'll be an easy target on horseback. You need to be in the truck with me."

"She's right, Sawyer. Besides, you need medical care as soon as possible. Take the truck and go," Clay said.

What Sawyer wanted was to catch the bastard that had shot him, the son of a bitch who had put such fear on Janis's face. But he knew Janis was right. He didn't need to make a target of himself and he trusted that if the man could be caught, Flint and Mac would catch him.

"I can't believe this happened," Janis said once they were in the truck and headed back.

"This wasn't exactly in my afternoon plans."

A sob escaped her. "You're bleeding a lot, Sawyer," she said through her tears. "My God, you could have been killed."

"But the good news is that I wasn't."

"How badly are you hurt?" She continued to softly cry.

"I probably just need a kiss and a bandage and I'll be fine," he said in an attempt to stop her tears.

It didn't work. She continued to weep as he pulled the truck to a halt by the big, two-story house where Cassie and Dillon lived.

Together they got out and he banged on the back door.

Cassie answered and gasped when she saw the blood coming from the gunshot wound.

She ushered them inside. "What happened?"

"Somebody shot him," Janis blurted and once again began to cry.

"You have some kind of a first-aid kit?" he asked. "And if Dillon isn't here, could you call him and get him here? Somebody just tried to kill me out in the pasture by the pond."

"Come with me." Cassie led them up the stairs and into the large master bathroom. She opened the linen closet and pulled out a first-aid kit.

"I'll help him," Janis said. She had stopped crying but still wore the shock of the horrible events on her pale features.

"I'll go back downstairs and call Dillon. I'm also calling Dr. Washington. You need to have a doctor look at that wound," Cassie replied.

Once she was gone, Sawyer winced as he shrugged out of his shirt.

Janis caught her lower lip with her teeth at the sight of the bloody mess.

"It's not as bad as it looks," he said in an effort to staunch any more tears.

"Sit," she commanded, pointing to the commode. She turned on the faucets in the sink and grabbed a cloth from the first-aid kit. She adjusted the water temperature, held the cloth beneath the spray and then began to clean up the blood.

"I'm glad you stopped crying," he said as she worked.

"I think I've moved from tears to complete and utter shock," she replied. "I just can't believe this happened."

Sawyer winced as she began to clean the wound itself. To take his mind off the pain, he focused on her…on the incredible length of her eyelashes and the gold flecks that kept her eyes from being a plain boring brown.

He concentrated on the light floral scent of her that he now identified as belonging to her alone and the shiny strands of her hair that he knew was soft and silky.

Lordy, but he wanted her. He'd wanted her when

her face had lit with excitement as she'd reeled in her fish. He'd wanted her when they were picnicking together. He wanted her now, even with pain racking his shoulder and her fighting back tears.

Maybe he should focus on the pain. He'd never felt this kind of sharp craving for a woman before. It had always been so easy for him to put the physical aspect of his relationships with other women on the back burner. However, there was something about Janis that had him fevered for her.

What he should be thinking about was who in the hell had held the gun that had shot at him. There was no doubt in his mind it was the same man who had written him the anonymous note warning him to stay away from her. It was the same person who had slashed his tire. But who was he?

Hopefully, Clay and the others would come back with the creep hog-tied to one of their saddles. He wanted the man in jail for attempted murder.

"At least I don't see a bullet," Janis murmured, her breath a warm caress on the side of his face. "And it looks like the bleeding has stopped."

"I told you I'd be fine with just a bandage and a kiss," he replied.

"We'll let Dr. Washington be the judge of that," she replied.

"Why? Is he going to kiss me?"

"Stop."

He looked at her innocently. "Stop what?"

"Stop trying to make me laugh. This isn't a laughing matter, Sawyer." Her lips trembled and she looked like new tears were just a blink away.

"You're right." He stood and waved away any further help from her. "Now all I need is a kiss from my woman and then we're going downstairs to wait for Dillon."

She didn't hesitate. She rose up on her tiptoes and gave him a gentle kiss filled with caring on his cheek. It was short and sweet but that didn't stop him from responding to it.

He grabbed his bloody shirt off the sink and together they headed down the stairs, where Dr. Eric Washington was already waiting for them.

Dr. Washington had been the town doctor in Bitterroot forever. He was far past retirement age, still made house calls, and told everyone who would listen that he'd retire when he was dead.

"Let's see what we have here." He motioned Sawyer into one of the chairs at the kitchen table and took off the bandage Janis had placed over the wound only moments before.

"Hmm, looks like a flesh wound that has been nicely cleaned," he said with approval. "Did you apply anything to it?"

"Some antibacterial cream," Janis replied.

"Good." Dr. Washington reapplied the bandage. "Keep applying the antibacterial cream and if it starts to look red and angry, come see me. I'll call in a prescription for some pain medication. You can pick it up at the pharmacy later this afternoon."

At that moment Dillon came in through the back door with Officer Ben Taylor at his side. "What's going on?" Dillon asked.

"I believe Janis's innocent stalker just tried to kill me," Sawyer replied.

"I'll just get out of here so you all can talk," Dr. Washington said.

"Send me the bill, Doc," Sawyer called out to him as the old man headed for the door.

Dr. Washington gave a wave over his head as he walked out the back door.

"Now, tell me exactly what happened," Dillon said.

Sawyer went over the events of the afternoon from them fishing to the moment the bullets had flown.

"Whoever it was didn't appear to be shooting at Janis. Thank God a couple of the men heard the gunfire and rode out to save us."

"Where are those men now?" Dillon asked.

"I'm assuming they're still out there looking for the creep," Sawyer replied and tried to ignore the pain shooting through his shoulder. Janis stood right behind him and he could feel her concern draping over him like a heavy cloth.

"What pasture?" Dillon asked.

"Down by the pond."

Dillon turned to look at Ben. "Head down there now and see what's going on."

With a nod, Ben disappeared out the back door.

Dillon pulled a small notepad from his slacks' pocket and made several notes.

"Tell me again exactly what happened," he said.

With a deep sigh, Sawyer went through the events of the day once again. There was something niggling at the back of Sawyer's mind, but he couldn't figure out what it was.

Dillon took more notes, stopping only when Clay and Ben came in through the back door.

"We searched everywhere, but all we found was a depressed area in the grass where the shooter must have sat waiting to get a good shot." Clay swept off his hat and released a deep sigh of frustration. "We really wanted to catch him, but he was obviously one step ahead of us."

"Did any of you hear a vehicle taking off?" Dillon asked.

Clay shook his head. "I asked all the other men if they'd seen a vehicle on the property, but nobody saw anything. He must have left on foot."

"He probably parked just up the road," Sawyer said.

For the next half an hour they talked about who might have been behind the gun, but no real suspects came to mind.

"Now that I know this person wants me dead, I'll

make sure to be a little more careful of where I go," Sawyer said as he got up from the table.

All he really wanted to do at the moment was to take Janis someplace where the two of them could relax. He didn't want her to have all this drama in her head when he took her home. He wanted her to have happy thoughts when she drifted off to sleep that night.

"If you need me, I'll be at the café with Janis, enjoying some great dessert and conversation," he said. He offered Janis a reassuring smile. "All I have to do is stop by my room and grab a clean shirt."

He threw his good arm around Janis's shoulder.

"Cassie, thanks for the first-aid kit," he said and then, together, he and Janis left the house.

They got into the pickup and he drove toward the cowboy bunkhouse.

"Sawyer, could we just call it a day? I really don't feel like going to the café or doing anything."

He stopped the truck and turned to look at her. "Are you sure?"

"Sawyer, you just got shot in the shoulder. An inch difference could have seen you dead. I thought we both were going to die out there. Sorry, but I just don't feel like sitting around in the café and eating dessert like nothing happened. I'm a little sick to my stomach and I really just want to go home."

"It was a dumb idea," he replied. "I was just trying

to salvage something good out of the day so that our time together would end on a better note."

"And I appreciate the thought," she replied.

He turned his truck around and headed for town. He didn't like the silence that rode with them. It was a weighty, close silence that made him nervous.

He cast a quick glance at Janis as they pulled into the small parking area behind the bar. Her shoulders were stiffened and her face still wore a sickly shade of pale.

Together they got out of the truck and he walked with her to the door. She pulled her key out of her purse and unlocked it.

She then turned around to look at him and the intensity of her gaze formed a ball of tension in the center of his chest.

"Sawyer, I like you. I like you a lot. But I don't want to go out with you anymore."

Chapter 6

Her heart was breaking, but she'd made up her mind. It didn't matter that Sawyer's eyes had darkened and his entire body had stiffened at her words.

"Can we talk about this inside?" he asked.

She immediately allowed him entry into the room. The last thing she wanted was for him to stand around outside where another bullet might find him.

"Janis, I like you, too. In fact, I like you better than any woman I've ever dated before. I feel like we're moving toward something really good. You can't stop it now."

Tears blurred her vision and she directed her gaze down to her feet. "I can't take a chance on your life, Sawyer. You got hurt today and it's all my fault."

"Don't you dare take the blame for what happened today," he replied with an edge of anger in his tone. "Whoever shot me is a nut. Are you're going to let some nut keep you away from me?"

"If it means saving your life, then the answer is yes." She wiped at her eyes and returned her gaze to him. The bandage was stark white against the bronzed skin of his bare chest. His hair was in disarray but shone with gold highlights woven into the copper color. He'd never looked as handsome, as sexy, as he did right now while she was telling him goodbye.

"Then are you willing to never date again for the rest of your life?" he asked. "Because I have a feeling this guy isn't going to just go away. He'll be a risk to any man you choose to date in the future."

"I don't care about that, all I care about is you," she said fervently. How could this be happening to her...to them? Who was this person who'd tried to kill Sawyer just for dating her?

Sawyer stepped closer to her, close enough that he reached out and stroked his fingers down the side of her face. She couldn't help the way her face turned into the caress even as her heart was breaking.

"Honey, don't let him win. I'm a big boy and I can take care of myself."

"But you were shot," she cried plaintively. "You could have been killed." The tears she'd been trying so hard to keep at bay slowly slid down her cheeks.

He nodded and dropped his hand to his side. "But, I wasn't. I don't intend to hang out in a pasture with you again until after this man is caught. As long as we're smart, we'll be all right. Just don't cut me out, Janis. Don't give up on us."

Her head told her to send him packing for his own good, but her heart wavered. She wanted to do the right thing, but why did it have to hurt so badly?

When he reached out to pull her into his arms, she tried to resist by stepping back from him. But he wouldn't be denied. He stepped forward and embraced her. She also couldn't help the way her arms wrapped around his neck as if they belonged there.

"I'm so afraid for you," she whispered into the crook of his neck.

"Whoever he is, he'll show his hand sooner or later. In the meantime we'll make sure we're either here or in a crowd when we do go out. It will be all right, Janis. Please, don't be afraid." His arms tightened around her. "For God's sake, give us a chance. Don't let this creep have his way and rip apart what's just beginning."

"Okay," she relented, hating herself for being so weak where he was concerned. She stepped out of his embrace. "But if you wind up dead, I'll never, ever, forgive you."

He grinned...the slightly crooked smile that warmed her heart. "Trust me, I'll be a little upset with myself if I wind up dead. And now I'm going to get out of here and let you get a good night's sleep."

"I think you're the one who needs some rest." Her gaze lingered on the bandage. "Don't forget to stop at the pharmacy and get your pain medication. You'll call somebody if you start to run a fever or if you don't feel right?"

"I promise I will. Good night, Janis. I'll see you tomorrow and we go forward with no regrets."

"No regrets," she repeated.

After he left, she got into a hot shower and cried with the residual fear of those moments when she'd been behind the truck and listening to the gunshots that she knew were directed at Sawyer.

No regrets, he'd said. Yet she couldn't help worrying that seeing Sawyer again after today was a huge mistake. But, God help her, she didn't want to stop seeing him.

Surely they could be safe if they were never out in public together without other people around. And there was no reason why they couldn't hang out in her room. She could even cook him dinner here, using the bar equipment on Sundays when the bar was closed.

They could be safe, couldn't they? But was that her head talking or her heart?

She got out of the shower, pulled on her nightshirt and, even though it was early, she got into bed. Immediately visions from the afternoon slashed through her mind.

The sudden pop… Sawyer slamming her to the ground and the horrifying knowledge that somebody was shooting at them… The acrid scent of Sawyer's gunfire filled her nose as fear accelerated her heartbeat…

Then there was the moment she'd seen his shoulder…the shirt ripped and bloody. She sat up, her heart racing so fast she could scarcely catch her breath. He was safe, she told herself. It was over and both of them had survived.

Who was responsible for this? What person did she know who was a potential murderer? What man wanted nobody else in her life? Or, was it possible it was a woman? It didn't matter. It was crazy. It was a sick game and somehow she needed to figure out who it was.

In the meantime she'd just have to wait to see how things played out. Sawyer seemed adamant that he didn't intend to go anywhere and she didn't know whether to be happy or horrified by his decision. All she knew for sure was that she was precariously close to falling in love with Sawyer Quincy.

As she stretched out once again in an effort to fall asleep, she had that creepy-crawly feeling again… like somebody was watching her.

Her curtains were pulled tightly closed, so nobody

could peek in. She looked at her closet door and then toward the bathroom.

There's nobody there, she told herself.

There wasn't anyone watching her. She was just feeling uneasy because of the events of the day and she was going to continue feeling uneasy until the person who was apparently stalking her and trying to kill Sawyer was caught.

Damn it!

He'd arrived in the woods in time to see Janis and Sawyer stretched out on a checkered tablecloth. The sight had stirred his anger into a near-blinding rage.

He knew he'd get a better shot at the cowboy if he patiently waited until they stood. But he feared what he'd be subjected to seeing before that happened.

It would be natural for the two of them to turn to each other…to passionately kiss…to possibly make love right there in front of him. He couldn't stand the thought, let alone the vision, of it happening.

And they had kissed. He'd had to momentarily look away from the sight of their desire. Thankfully the kiss hadn't lasted for long.

Janis was his, and that big, dumb cowboy didn't have a right to touch her in any way. He had no right to kiss her.

He'd watched the two of them together until he couldn't stand it any longer.

His gun had burned in his hand, as if the fever

of his rage had infected it. He'd aimed at Sawyer's head and had fired, cursing when the bullet missed the target.

The attempt to kill Sawyer had been a dismal failure, and he'd been cursing himself ever since. The best thing he could hope for was that Sawyer would be afraid for his life and would stop seeing Janis. That was the only way he'd get to stay alive.

As for Janis, his plans for her were nearly complete. Excitement rocketed through him. Soon she would belong to him and only him.

Sawyer leaned back in his saddle and surveyed the herd of Black Angus cattle before him. He was looking for any sick or wounded. These cows were the bread and butter of the ranch and, as such, they received a lot of care.

The other men had tried to talk him into taking the day off. Even though his shoulder was still sore, it wasn't bad enough to lay him up.

Besides, he liked working hard. Cassie paid them a fair wage. All the men had good work ethics and it wasn't just about a paycheck, it was about their emotional connection to the ranch where they had all grown up.

Clay was on horseback next to him and they'd only been out in the pasture five minutes before Clay urged him to go back to the stables.

"You're a target on that horse," he said. "Go in and

clean some equipment in the barn, or polish some leather in the stables."

"I'm not going to change the way I live my life because of some nutcase," he replied.

"That nutcase almost killed you yesterday," Clay said. "You got lucky it was just your shoulder that took a bullet. It could have easily been your head or your heart."

"Yeah, I know. But what am I supposed to do? Hole up someplace and shiver in my boots with fear? Should I stop seeing a woman I think might be my future happiness?" Sawyer heaved a deep sigh.

"I don't know, man. I'm just worried if you keep sitting on that horse you won't have a future at all," Clay replied.

"I'm hoping this guy will slip up, that he'll do something stupid and Dillon will be able catch him."

"Yeah, but in the meantime none of us feel good about you being out on horseback in the pasture," Clay replied.

Sawyer suddenly realized he wasn't just putting himself at risk, he was also putting at risk the lives of the men he considered his brothers. A bullet aimed at Sawyer could just as easily go awry and slam into anyone near him. The last thing he wanted was to put somebody else in danger.

"Okay, point taken," he said to Clay. "I'm heading in. I'm sure Flint will be thrilled if I take over his job of mucking out stalls for the day."

"Good decision, Sawyer. We all want to keep you alive," Clay replied.

Minutes later Sawyer was in the stables and cleaning out stalls. As he worked, his mind buzzed with the questions that had plagued him since the night he'd found the note on his windshield.

Who was this person? What was his ultimate goal? What in God's creation was his end game? Was it simply to make sure Janis never got close to a man? Or was it something even more ominous?

There was still something that niggled in the back of his brain, something he felt was vitally important. But he couldn't, for the life of him, figure out what it was.

It was still bothering him when he walked into the dining room that evening where the scent of roast beef filled the air, along with the talk and laughter of the men already there.

Meals were served buffet style and Cookie never made a bad dish. The beef stew held chunks of tender meat and carrots and potatoes. There was also coleslaw, big corn muffins and some kind of a marshmallow fruit salad.

"How's the shoulder?" Jerod asked as he fell into line behind Sawyer.

"Sore, but I'll survive. How's the volunteer work going?"

Jerod had recently started volunteering at the

Bitterroot community center, working with the local youth.

"I'm really enjoying it. You'd be surprised by how many kids there are here in town who don't have a great home life. My goal is to keep them from becoming runaways like we all were."

"Yeah, there aren't many people like Big Cass around. We got lucky winding up here. Unfortunately most runaways don't get so lucky."

They filled their plates and then joined the others at one of the picnic tables. The usual joking and laughter accompanied the meal, but Sawyer was only half engaged by the conversations around him.

Instead his mind went over and over everything that had happened since the night the bar had been spray-painted. He was missing something… Something important.

His mind was still working overtime as he drove into town to spend the evening at the Watering Hole. His heart had nearly stopped last night when Janis had said she didn't want to see him anymore.

He really believed they were building something wonderful between them and he was sick at the idea that it would all be destroyed because of some anonymous creep. The last thing he wanted to do was to put her in any danger, but he was certain the perp didn't want to harm her whether she was seeing Sawyer or not. He was the target, and he'd take the risk. He'd become invested in her and she was worth it.

The bar was relatively busy when he walked in at just after seven. He instantly spied Janis working the bar. His heart lifted at the warm smile she greeted him with.

He slid onto one of the empty bar stools and returned her smile. "How's your shoulder doing?" she asked, her brown eyes darkening with concern.

"It's fine. It's gonna take more than a single bullet to get me down." His attempt at a little humor didn't lighten her eyes back to their normal shade of rich caramel. "Janis, I'm fine," he assured her. "How are you?"

"A little tired. It took me a long time to fall asleep last night." She fixed him his usual soda and lime and then continued. "I know it sounds crazy, but I kept feeling like somebody was watching me."

"I'm sorry. I know this is all difficult for you," he replied. "The last thing I want is for you to feel uncomfortable in your own space."

"I'd question my sanity if I didn't have some sort of reaction to what happened yesterday," she replied. "Did you pick up your pain meds?"

"Nah, I'm fine without them," he replied.

Their conversation was interrupted by Myles Hennessy. "Hey, darlin', I thought you were my girl," he called from the other end of the bar. "Are you going to let that cowboy monopolize all your time?"

"No, only part of my time," she replied. "I'll be

right back," she told Sawyer before she walked to the other end of the bar to take care of Myles.

Myles Hennessy. Did he really believe Janis was his girl? Was his flirting truly harmless fun? Was it possible he was the man they were looking for? A person who had hidden in the woods and tried to kill Sawyer?

Or was it John Bailey? The fortysomething sat at the end of the bar, his dark eyes brooding as he drank his whiskey. John had never married. As far as Sawyer knew, the man didn't even date. Was it because he'd harbored a secret crush on Janis?

Then there was Damon West, also seated on a stool at the bar. Had the widower honed in on Janis as his next bride? They were the same men he'd looked at before, but this time he was looking for a man who had murder in his heart.

These three men almost always sat at the bar or in a section Janis was working. Sawyer frowned and took a sip of his drink. Hell, the perp could be any one of them or any other man who frequented the bar.

The night wore on and still something continued to bother him. What was it? What clue might he have in the depths of his brain that refused to surface?

It was almost closing time when the thing that had been bothering him came into clear focus. He motioned to Janis, who was at the other end of the bar serving Myles another drink.

"Who did you tell we were going to fish and have a picnic before we went?" he asked her.

She frowned thoughtfully. "I might have mentioned it to Annie, but other than her, nobody."

"And I didn't even tell the other men on the ranch that I was taking you out there for a picnic. Other than Cookie, nobody else knew." A tight knot formed in the pit of his stomach.

"Then how did the man know we'd be out there?" she asked. "How did he know we'd be out there on that day and at that time?" Her eyes got larger… darker.

"The only place we talked about our plans was in your room." The knot in his stomach tightened. "That means the only way the man knew to be in those woods at that time of the afternoon was because there's a listening device in your room." He watched as a new horror filled her eyes.

Chapter 7

"A listening device?" Janis echoed his words in an effort to make sense of them. Who on earth would be listening to her when she was in the privacy of her own place? The hair on the nape of her neck rose as goose bumps raced up and down her arms. It was too creepy to even digest.

"As soon as you're finished out here, we're going to rip your room apart until we find it," Sawyer said.

For the next hour she waited on customers and made small talk, but her mind buzzed with the new, horrifying information. A listening device. Was it really possible?

Had she told anyone about the fishing date? No, she listened to the patrons, but she never shared her own personal business with any of them. And she wasn't even sure she'd told Annie. So, how would anyone know they were going to be in that pasture?

If there really was some sort of listening device in her room, how long had it been there? What did the person who had planted it hope to hear? The sound of her breathing at night? Her singing slightly off-key while she thumbed through her wish book? Maybe that's what had given her that creepy-crawly feeling.

Surely there had to be another explanation. Maybe she had mentioned it to Annie and then Annie had told somebody about their plans. Even as the thought entered her mind, she dismissed it. Why on earth would Annie tell anyone what Janis and Sawyer were doing on a Sunday afternoon?

Time couldn't move fast enough, but finally it was closing time and she and Sawyer were the only two people left in the bar. She locked the front door and then, together, they walked toward the back of the bar and through the door that led to her private quarters.

"I'm really hoping you're wrong," she said. "I hope we don't find anything because otherwise it's just way too creepy."

"It is creepy," he agreed.

He'd been able to joke when he'd taken a bullet to the shoulder, but there was no sign of his humor right now. His body was tensed and his mouth was a thin slash. He looked bigger and more serious than she'd ever seen him as he sat on her bed and picked up her landline phone.

He unscrewed both the earpiece and the mouthpiece. His deepening frown told her he'd found nothing that shouldn't be there. He put it back together and then looked around the room, his eyes narrowed and his gaze intent.

She did the same thing, seeking someplace where a bug could be hidden. "Maybe the overhead light?" she asked.

"Maybe," he replied. "I need to get a stool from the bar in order to check it out."

As he left to go into the other room, Janis sank down on the bed and checked out her bedside lamp. She couldn't believe this was happening. Surely they were mistaken. Maybe Annie really had mentioned their plans in passing to somebody.

The bedside lamp held nothing suspicious and by that time Sawyer was back with a stool. He appeared even more tense than he'd been before. He climbed on top of the stool and unfastened the screws holding the frosted glass dome cover. "Nothing," he said in disgust and then set to putting the dome back in place.

When he was finished, he moved the stool to check out the smoke alarm. He pulled off the white cover and checked it out. "Bingo," he said softly as he removed a small piece of electronics.

"Oh, my God, I can't believe it," she said with

a stunned gasp. Her heart beat so hard she feared it might explode. Somebody had been bugging her room. Her mind struggled to wrap around that fact. Why? And, more importantly, who?

Sawyer climbed down off the stool and sat next to her on the bed. He placed the offending object on the floor and smashed it with his boot. He hit it once…twice…three times and then turned to face her. His features were grim as he held her gaze for a long moment. Her heart began to beat with a new anxious rhythm. "What?" she asked.

"I have worse news."

She stared at him, wondering what on earth could be worse than having her privacy being violated by a listening device. "Tell me." The words whispered out of her as the back of her throat tightened up.

"There are peepholes in your wall."

She stared at him, trying to comprehend what he had just said. Had she misunderstood him? Peepholes? Then the utter shock of clear realization shuttered through her. "Holes in the wall?" she echoed. Suddenly she was ice-cold and her stomach roiled with nausea. "Show me."

They got off the bed and walked across the room to the wall that separated her room from the bar. He ran his hand across the faded pink-flowered wallpaper. "Here." He took her trembling hand and guided it to a spot that appeared to be the dark center of a flower.

"And here." He pulled her to the left and ran her fingers across another hole in the wall. The horror inside her grew to near screaming proportions as he found yet another…and another one.

Somebody had sat on the other side of the wall and watched her as she'd dressed and undressed. Standing next to Sawyer, she felt naked and dirty.

"The bathroom," she said as a new horror shivered through her. They found two more holes in the bathroom wall, one of them in the shower.

Some pervert had seen her naked in the shower and while she'd done other personal business. She began to hyperventilate as sobs choked out of her.

Sawyer pulled her out of the bathroom and wrapped her in his strong arms. She leaned against him, her legs almost too shaky to hold her up. He seemed to sense that and he held her tight enough that she couldn't fall.

"It's going to be all right," he whispered, stroking his hand up and down her back as she wept uncontrollably.

How was anything ever going to be all right again? Unbeknownst to her, she'd been somebody's personal peep show. It was absolutely horrifying.

"He…he could be watching us now…right this minute," she gasped. She shoved against him, needing to escape this room that had once been home and now felt like an evil, alien place. "I've got to get out of here."

"Grab a sweater and we'll go outside. I'll call Dillon."

"No, we can't do that," she said. "What if he's just waiting for you to go outside where he can shoot you again?"

"We'll be fine," he assured her. "And nobody was in the bar. Let's get out of here at least until Dillon arrives."

A few moments later she had a white sweater pulled tightly around her despite the warmth of the night. Sawyer had called Dillon and now they just waited for the lawman to arrive.

She'd finally stopped crying but remained shocked and appalled by what had been discovered. How long had the holes been there? Who was behind them, peeking in at her? The whole thing was so tawdry, so revolting.

"It has to be somebody I work with," she finally said as the initial horror began to fade away and she began to think more clearly.

"I thought it was somebody who came into the bar all the time, but I think you're right. It's got to be somebody you work with. One of the holes was in the back wall of the bar, but two of them were in the storage closet and the other two would be in the kitchen."

The names and faces of all the men she worked with flashed through her head at dizzying speed. These were men she would have trusted with her life, and yet one of them was a perverted creep who had not only watched her in her most private moments, but had also tried to kill Sawyer.

He threw an arm over her shoulder and pulled her close against his side. "You are not spending another night in this place until we get to the bottom of things," he said.

The assurance in his voice was comforting, but there was only one problem. "I don't have any place else to go."

"You can't stay with your mother for a little while?"

She stiffened. "I refuse to stay with that woman for a single night."

"Then I'll arrange for a room for you at the motel," he replied.

"At least there I'll know nobody is watching me." She remembered all the nights she'd gotten that crazy crawly feeling that somebody was watching her. Now she knew it hadn't just been her imagination. It had been real…so horrifyingly real. "We probably should call Gary. He needs to know about all this, too."

Before she could put action to words, Dillon pulled in.

"I'm seeing you two way too much lately," he said in greeting.

"I hope I never see you again under these kinds of circumstances," Janis replied.

"You mentioned when you called something about

a listening device and peepholes in the wall?" Dillon looked at Sawyer.

Sawyer nodded and then looked at her. "You want to wait out here?"

"No, I'll come in with you two and start packing a suitcase," she replied. She couldn't wait to get to the motel. Being in that room made her almost physically ill.

As Sawyer showed Dillon the holes and the crushed listening device, she pulled a large suitcase out of the closet and placed it open on her bed. She fought back a new round of tears as she folded clothes and placed them in the suitcase.

Dillon called Gary and she was almost all packed by the time he arrived. His burly body and energy instantly filled the room. But when he saw the peepholes, his anger shot through the ceiling.

"Who the hell is responsible for this?" he asked rhetorically. "What kind of nasty crap is this and how do we find out who did it?" He looked at Dillon and then turned toward Janis. "Honey, I can't tell you how sorry I am. I swear, if I find out who it is, I'll wring his damned neck."

"You'll have to beat me to him," Sawyer said grimly. "As soon as we finish up here, I'm taking Janis to the motel."

Gary nodded. "And don't worry, Janis. If you need some time off, we'll work that out," he said. "Whatever you need, Janis. Just let me know."

"Right now I don't know what I need," she replied. She was lost in a world she suddenly didn't understand, one that was fraught with uncertainty and fear.

Dillon looked at Gary. "I'd like you to call a full staff meeting first thing in the morning. I want to talk to everyone who works here."

Gary nodded. "I can make that happen. How about eight in the morning?"

"Works for me," Dillon said. "And we'll discuss how we're going to handle things then."

"I will be here at eight, too," Sawyer said firmly.

"And I'll be with you," she replied and grabbed his hand. His fingers curled warmly around hers. She had a feeling she could face almost anything in the world if he was right by her side.

"For now, let's keep this a secret," Dillon said. "I would prefer you don't talk about it to anyone else."

"If I had my way, I'd never tell anyone that this happened," she replied. It was so embarrassing.

"You got my word, it stays here between just us," Gary said.

She looked at one of the peepholes and a wild, hollow wind blew through her. Why her? Why had somebody developed this obsessive desire for her?

Because you're a whore, the strident voice whispered in her brain. *You'll always be a whore.*

"No," she said aloud and then flushed when she realized the men were looking at her. "Can we go now?" she asked Dillon. More than anything, she needed to escape this room.

He nodded his assent. It took her only a couple of minutes to pack up most of her toiletries and be ready to leave.

They left by the front door of the bar where Sawyer's truck was parked just outside. He carried her suitcase, placed it in the back, and they were on their way to the motel.

The darkness of the night couldn't begin to compete with the darkness in her soul. She felt dirty... tainted in a way she'd never dreamed possible.

"I think I will take a couple of days off work," she said as a deep weariness overtook her.

"I think I'm going to take a couple of days off, too. I'll carry in some meals for you and we can spend some time together."

She looked at him in surprise. "Oh, Sawyer, you can't do that," she protested.

"You don't want to spend more time with me?"

"Well, of course, I do. But—"

"Then it's settled. Besides, I'm a gunshot victim. I could use a couple of days off."

His words instantly pulled her out of her own head. "Are you hurting? Is there anything I can do to help?"

"I could think of a few things you could do to make me feel better." He slid her that sexy smile that, just for a moment, made everything bad go away.

"Are you thinking naughty thoughts?"

A small laugh escaped him. "Guilty as charged."

The lightness lasted only a moment. As he turned into the motel parking lot the darkness of her situation slammed back into her.

Together they got out of the truck and went into the motel office where owner Fred Ferguson greeted them. "Need a room for the night?" he asked, his gaze speculative as he looked first at Janis and then at Sawyer.

"Janis needs a room for about a week," Sawyer said. "And the fewer people who know she's here, the better." He knew Fred was a gossiper, but Sawyer could only hope he wouldn't gossip about Janis staying here or spread a rumor that Sawyer and Janis were shacking up together.

Fred frowned. "Are you expecting some kind of trouble?"

"Not at all," Sawyer replied. He glanced at the woman standing next to him. She worried him. He couldn't imagine how she felt knowing that some bastard had been watching her in her most private moments for who knew how long. At the moment, she was too pale and far too quiet not to worry him.

Her tears were normal under the circumstances. Even the momentary levity had felt normal. But her silence and the haunted look in her eyes was worrisome.

For the first time in his life he desperately wished

he owned a house, a place where he could take her and she'd feel completely safe. But he didn't have a house and the motel was the only answer for her at the moment.

Fred told her a price but it was Sawyer who pulled out a credit card to pay.

"Sawyer," she protested.

"Shh," he returned. "This week is on me."

He paid and Fred shoved a key on a plastic key-ring toward him. "Unit seven," he said. "It's on the south end of the building."

Minutes later Sawyer carried her suitcase into the room. All the rooms were housekeeping units so, besides the king-size bed, there was also a stove, a sink and a fridge. There was a small kitchen table and an easy chair next to the door. The most important thing was that there were no peepholes in the place.

"Home sweet home," he said and set the suitcase just inside the door.

She went to the windows and looked them over and then checked the door where there was not only a regular door lock but also a sturdy dead bolt. When she turned to face Sawyer, her face displayed a dark, haunted look that almost broke his heart.

"Janis," he said softly and then gathered her into his arms. She leaned into him and held tight, as if he was the only person on the planet that could keep her safe. And he wanted to be that man for her.

He'd always been easygoing and satisfied with

where he was in life. He'd never wanted to be more for anyone until now. But, as he held Janis in his arms and felt her heart beating against his own, he wanted more from himself for her. But at this moment there was nothing he could do to make the situation better.

Reluctantly he released her and she stepped back from him. "Do you want me to stay here with you tonight?"

She hesitated and then straightened her shoulders. "No, I'll be fine. But could you stay just a little bit longer?"

"Darlin', I'll stay for as long as you need me."

She smiled at him gratefully. "I see there is a coffeepot with all the trimmings. Why don't I make us each a cup of coffee?"

"Sounds good to me. While you're doing that, I'll put your suitcase up on the bed where it will be easier for you to unpack," he replied.

He hefted the suitcase on top of the bed then sat in the chair near the door and watched as she made the coffee. When the fragrant brew began to drip into the glass carafe, she sat on the edge of the bed, facing him.

"I keep thinking of all the men I work with at the bar and wondering which one of them is guilty," she said.

"Is there any of them who, in retrospect, gave

you the willies or has acted inappropriately around you?" he asked.

"That's just it, none of them has ever made me feel uncomfortable, but I know it has to be somebody connected with the bar. He'd have to be spying on me when the bar was closed and that means whoever it is has a key to the place."

"Do you know specifically who has a key?" he asked. At least some of the color had returned to her face and she appeared more animated than she'd been minutes before.

"Gary has always been quite generous when handing out keys. I'm sure all of the kitchen help has one and, of course, James Warner has one since he works as a janitor for the place."

"And two of those peepholes were located in the janitorial closet," he replied. A wealth of anger rose up inside him as he thought of some man sitting in that closet and watching Janis undress.

He'd heard about voyeurs before, but he'd never understood it, nor did he want to. All he wanted was to catch the sick bastard.

"Sit tight," he said and jumped to his feet. "I'll get the coffee."

He needed to do something to rid himself of the growing rage over everything that had happened. He poured the coffee into the two foam cups provided. He handed hers to her and then sat back down in the chair.

"What I'm hoping is that whoever it is will show their guilt on their face when confronted tomorrow morning at the meeting," he said.

"That would definitely be nice, although I'm not getting my hopes up," she replied. She took a sip of coffee then set the cup on the nightstand.

"I should really start to unpack," she said without moving. She released a tired sigh. "Now that the initial shock and horror is over, I'm completely exhausted."

"Then I should get out of here so you can unpack and get into bed." He drained his coffee in three big swigs and then walked the cup to the trash can.

By that time she was on her feet. Sawyer couldn't ever remember being so reluctant to leave a woman before. She walked with him to the door and once again he wrapped her in an embrace.

He breathed in the sweet scent of her hair and a fierce protectiveness surged inside him. "I'm so sorry you're going through all this," he said softly. "If I could, I'd take it all away."

She raised her head and looked at him, her lips trembling slightly. "I'm still mostly afraid for you. I mean, this person hasn't tried to harm me physically, but he shot you."

"I'll be okay," he replied. "This creep isn't going to keep me from you, no matter what happens."

Her eyes warmed and her lips opened with invitation.

He covered her mouth with his, loving the taste of her and the way she fit so neatly against his body.

Before the kiss could become something more, he released her. "Are you sure you still want to go to the meeting in the morning? You really don't have to be there."

"But I want to be there," she said with a resolute raise of her chin. "I need to look each and every man there square in their eyes."

"Then I'll pick you up about quarter to eight in the morning," he replied.

"I should have had my wits about me to drive my car here from the bar."

"I'd prefer you keep your car at the bar," he replied. "If you need to go anywhere or do anything I'll be available to you 24/7."

"How did I get so lucky?"

"I'm the lucky one," he replied and kissed her on the forehead. He didn't dare kiss her on the lips again for he feared the combustible desire that would leap to life.

And the timing wasn't right tonight. He didn't want their first lovemaking to be marred by the ugliness of everything they had discovered.

She was getting over a shock. She was exhausted and looked like a poor, hurt puppy that wanted to be left alone to lick her wounds.

"Good night, Janis. See you in the morning," he

said, and then minutes later he was in his pickup and headed back to the Holiday Ranch.

He wasn't worried about her safety tonight. Only a couple of people knew where she was and the guilty party didn't know yet that they now knew about the peepholes.

Still, even telling himself she was okay, a knot of tension pressed tight against his chest. He knew he was in danger of being killed by the nutcase behind the peepholes and he intended to do everything in his power to see that didn't happen.

What worried him much more than his own safety was hers. She was right, so far the perp hadn't made any move to hurt her. It would be easy to write him off as a harmless voyeur indulging in his obsession. Janis.

But it was that obsession that scared Sawyer. What would happen when the voyeur discovered he could no longer watch Janis at the bar? Would that obsession turn to anger? To a rage directed at her? Would this escalate to something terrible that nobody could control? He didn't know.

He didn't want her to know that he was now worried about her safety. He'd wanted her to get a good night's sleep. Hopefully tomorrow they would be able to identify the guilty party and all would be well. However, if that didn't happen, then he feared tonight might just be the last good night's sleep either of them got.

Chapter 8

All the suspects were in the process of gathering in the bar for the early morning staff meeting. Janis sat next to Sawyer on the stools. Gary had come in early and had arranged the lower chairs that normally surrounded tables in a theater seating. He and Dillon stood in front of the group of chairs.

Before anyone arrived, Dillon had told them he was not going to mention anything about the peepholes. Rather, he was going to conduct interviews about Sawyer's shooting. After the interviews, he would talk to the group about how they would proceed next. Although she wanted the peepholes to be investigated, she had to trust that Dillon knew what he was doing.

He'd also told them that he'd attempted to lift fingerprints around the peepholes. But because the walls had been greasy from the kitchen and rough with the textured wallpaper that gave the appearance of wood planks, he hadn't been able to lift anything usable.

She now watched as each person entered the building. Had James Warner, the janitor, sat in that closet and watched her? Or had it been Miguel who cooked terrific food and was always ready with a smile?

Annie came in, along with Melissa Severn. The two were roommates and definitely not on Janis's potential suspect list. They were followed by head cook, Charlie Williams, and bartender Tanner Woodson.

Each time another person came in, the knot of tension twisted tighter in her stomach. Occasionally, Sawyer rubbed her back as if aware of the anxiety that ricocheted through her.

She hadn't slept well at all the night before. It had taken her forever to finally fall asleep and when she had, her sleep had been haunted by faceless monsters who chased her through the long night.

She was hoping for some sort of closure to happen this morning. She wanted the person stalking her, the person who had hurt Sawyer, arrested and thrown into jail…forever.

It wasn't until eight fifteen that everyone was

gathered and Dillon called for their attention. "Raise your hand if you have a key to this place."

Nearly everyone in the room raised a hand. "Everybody get your keys out so I can collect them all," Gary said.

Questions began to fly as Gary moved among them picking up the keys. Had something happened? Had items been stolen? What was going on?

Janis watched each person carefully, looking for any sign of discomfort, of guilt. She was certain that her stalker was in this room, but who was he?

"You know I need a key, Gary," Charlie protested. "I'm in here all hours of the day to check the food supplies and to take care of the meats I slow-cook. I also get deliveries early in the mornings before the bar is open."

Janis stared at the dark-haired man. She knew he wasn't married and lived alone just outside the city limits in the house he'd inherited when his mother and father had died. While he was coming in and out of the bar to check on his food, was he also sliding up to one of the holes in the wall to watch her? The thought sickened her.

"And you know I need a key," James Warner protested. "How am I supposed to get in here to clean the place up overnight if I don't have a key?" He looked at Gary and then slid a quick glance at Janis before once again looking at the owner of the place.

Her blood froze. James was in his early sixties

and had worked as a janitor/maintenance man here for the last ten years or so. He'd never been married and, as far as she knew, he didn't date. He'd have the tools to make those holes in the wall.

Whoever had made those holes was also fairly proficient with a gun. Not only had one of them watched her, but that same person had nearly killed Sawyer. Damn it, who was responsible? Who had a sick obsession for her?

"We'll figure out the key situation before everyone leaves here today," Gary said.

"Now, I'm taking you one at a time into Gary's office for some questioning," Dillon said.

"I can't hang around here all day," James protested, as did several of the others.

"Then I'll take you back first," Dillon replied.

As the two disappeared into Gary's office, the bar exploded with questions. Annie got up out of her chair and beelined to Janis and Sawyer.

"Do you guys know what's going on?" she asked.

Janis hesitated. "Yes, I know a few things," she admitted. But without knowing specifically what Dillon was telling people, she added, "But I can't talk about them right now."

"Oh, come on. You can tell me." Annie leaned closer to her.

"Annie, she can't," Sawyer said firmly.

"Then at least tell me this…am I in trouble?"

"No, not at all," Janis replied. "Just go in and answer Dillon's questions and you'll be fine."

"Getting any vibes from anyone?" Sawyer leaned over and whispered as Annie went back to her chair.

"Not really," she replied.

He rubbed her back and the only thing she knew with certainty was how much she appreciated Sawyer's strength, his support, in all of this.

Despite the lingering scents of fried food and the disinfectant James used to clean, Sawyer's cologne was a welcoming, familiar scent that made her feel safe.

As everyone else chatted with each other, Janis watched all the men carefully. Who in the room was not only an obsessive voyeur but also a potential killer? He had to be here. He had to have a key to get inside and that meant he had to be there right now.

When James came out of the office, he was pummeled with questions by the others. He shook his head and moved toward the front door. "The chief said he'd arrest me if I said anything to anyone, so I'm out of here."

Dillon appeared in the office doorway. "Charles," he said.

And so the morning went, with Dillon calling people into the office. It was nearly noon when he was finished and he and Gary and Janis and Sawyer were the only people left in the bar.

"I wish I could tell you I've identified the guilty person, but I can't," Dillon said.

"There wasn't anyone who appeared shady?" Sawyer asked.

"Actually, there were a couple. James and Rusty," he replied.

Janis wasn't surprised by him mentioning James, but she was completely surprised by him naming Rusty. Rusty Bratton was an older man who worked in the kitchen. He always had a friendly smile and was a hard worker.

"Neither of them had alibis for the day Sawyer was shot. Both of them definitely appeared like they had something to hide," Dillon said.

"Did you talk to them about the peepholes?" Janis asked.

"No, not specifically. I told them all that I want a written, detailed report of their activities for the past week on my desk by tomorrow morning." Dillon frowned thoughtfully. "I didn't want to tip our hand by telling them the peepholes had been discovered."

"I'm going to get Jesse St. John over here to fill the holes," Gary said. Jesse owned a business of home repair and remodeling.

Dillon frowned thoughtfully. "No, I don't want the holes disturbed. I don't want to show our hand to this snake."

"He's worse than a snake," Sawyer replied and rubbed his shoulder.

"I'd like you to move back into the room in the next couple of days," Dillon said to Janis. "I know it will be difficult, but if you aren't there, then our perp won't have a reason to sneak in here to look at you."

Janis's stomach churned at the very thought of going back to that room. It had been her home, her security, but it would never be home for her again.

"That's a lot to ask of her," Sawyer protested, his hand finding hers and squeezing tightly.

"I realize that. But we'll coordinate it so I'm hiding out in here during the nights." He looked at Gary. "I'm assuming you wouldn't have a problem with that."

"Not at all. Do whatever it takes to get the bastard arrested."

Dillon returned his gaze to Janis. "Then it's all up to you."

"I'll do it," she heard herself say.

"Are you sure?" Sawyer asked, his copper-colored eyes holding her gaze.

She slowly nodded and then looked at Dillon. "I'll do it because I want this person caught and jailed. If he isn't peeping at me, then he'll find some other poor woman to peep at." An icy cold clutched her heart. "Just give me a couple of days at the motel, and I'd like you to take me off the work schedule for that time."

"That can be done," Gary agreed.

"What are you going to tell everyone as to why she's out of the room now?" Sawyer asked.

"Bugs," Gary said. "I'll take the time before she comes back to fumigate her room. We'll tell everyone she was overrun by bugs."

"That will work," Dillon agreed.

"I'll make sure everyone gets their keys back today." Gary turned as Tanner came through the front door for the second time that morning.

"Is it business as usual today?" he asked. "If so, then my shift already started."

Gary looked at Dillon, who nodded and got out of his chair. "It's business as usual," Gary replied. "Help me get these chairs back where they belong."

"I'll help with that," Sawyer said.

Fifteen minutes later Janis and Sawyer were back in his truck. "How about we catch lunch at the café?"

"That sounds fine," she said, although her heart was still in her throat at the idea of going back to her room. How was she going to dress and use the bathroom knowing that somebody might be looking at her?

"Janis, you don't have to go back there," he said softly, as if he'd read her mind. "We'll figure out another way to catch him."

"Yes I do," she replied. She clutched her fingers tight in her lap, not wanting him to see that they trembled with anxiety. "I want to know who shot you. I need to know who this twisted person is, and

I think Dillon is right. This might be the only way to catch him."

She didn't even want to think about what she might possibly endure in an effort to reveal a person who would kill to keep her all to himself.

"You look exhausted," Sawyer said as they got out of his truck in front of the motel. They had just eaten a big lunch at the café where, thankfully, nobody had bothered them or asked them questions about what was going on at the Watering Hole.

She got the motel room key out of her purse and unlocked the door. "To be honest, I'm totally exhausted. I didn't get much sleep last night and I was so tense through the morning."

"Why don't I get out of here and let you get in a long nap," he said.

Her eyes were dark as she held his gaze. "Stay with me for a little while? Hold me while I sleep?"

"Darlin', I can't think of anything I'd rather do," he replied. Well, truth be told, he could think of one thing he'd like to do, but she hadn't invited him to make love to her. She'd merely asked him to hold her while she slept.

"I'm going to change out of these jeans and put on something more comfy," she said. She opened a drawer and pulled out a pair of gray jogging pants and a pink T-shirt. "I'll be right back." She disappeared into the bathroom.

He turned on the small bedside lamp and turned off the glaring overhead light. He then sat on the edge of the bed with a sigh. He hadn't slept much the night before, either. He'd tossed and turned, worry for her keeping sleep at bay.

He'd never known such admiration for a woman. The fact that she'd agreed to move back into the room in the bar had amazed him. Only an incredibly strong woman would make that choice.

He turned as she came out of the bathroom, looking small and vulnerable in the sweats and the oversize T-shirt. He put his gun and his cell phone on the nightstand, stretched out on the gold bedspread and beckoned her into his arms.

She turned off the bedside lamp and the room was lit only with stray beams of sunshine that danced in through a crack in the curtains.

She crawled up next to him and curled herself so he could spoon her with an arm thrown over her middle.

Her hair smelled like sunshine and flowers and her body fit neatly against his.

He hoped like hell he could keep his lustful thoughts of her at bay, but he knew it was going to be difficult with her so intimately close to him.

"Sawyer." Her drowsy voice let him know she was on the verge of sleep.

"Yes?" he replied.

"Thank you," she said.

"What are you thanking me for?" he asked.

"For being you."

His heart swelled with a happiness he'd never known before in his life. And it was at that moment he realized he was definitely in love with Janis Little.

It had happened so quickly, but it felt so right. She was the woman he'd been searching for to complete his life, to fill his future. The realization of his feelings for her filled him with awe. He wanted to wake her up right now and tell her how much he loved her, but he didn't.

He didn't know what she felt for him. Oh, he knew he was her safety net for now. There was no question she trusted him more than anyone else in her life. But that didn't necessarily equate to love.

Besides, maybe what he felt for her was just a healthy dose of lust and, once that was satisfied, his feelings for her wouldn't be quite as strong.

In any case, now wasn't the time to speak of his love for her. He would tell her how he felt about her when this nastiness was all resolved. He'd tell her when fear no longer darkened her eyes, when the relief of an arrest made their future happiness assured.

All he had to hope for was that she had or would fall in love with him. That was his last thought before he drifted off to asleep.

He awakened to soft, warm fingers dancing down the sides of his face. He opened his eyes to see Janis facing him, a soft smile playing on her features.

Instantly blood surged in every vein in his body. Did she have any idea what she was doing to him? Just looking at her made him want her. He'd never had this kind of hunger for a woman in his life.

"I didn't know how long you wanted to sleep," she said.

"What time is it?" he asked.

"It's just after six."

"Whew, I can't believe I slept this long."

She smiled. "We both must have needed it."

Her fingers once again stroked the side of his face, her eyes a deep caramel color that drew him in. He reached out and ran his fingers over her features like a blind man wanting to recognize…to memorize her.

"Kiss me, Sawyer," she whispered.

There was no way he was going to deny her request. He leaned forward and covered her lips with his. As always, her mouth was warm and inviting and, within seconds, he deepened the kiss.

His tongue danced with hers, instantly creating a flame deep inside him. She moved closer to him, her body pressed against his. She had to know that he was fully aroused. He couldn't help the way his body reacted to hers. Still, she had only asked for a kiss and nothing more.

As they continued to kiss, her breaths quickened, as did his own. Her hands tangled in his hair and he fought against a wildness growing inside him.

His hands caressed up and down her back. There

was nothing he wanted more than to take her T-shirt off so he was touching her bare skin. But he tamped down the wild desire.

The last thing he wanted to do was to somehow pressure her to do something she wasn't ready for. She had to have the lead and right now he would follow her anywhere.

As the kiss finally ended, her eyes had darkened to the color of rich chocolate. "Make love to me, Sawyer."

His heart nearly beat out of his chest as he held her gaze intently. "Are you sure? Janis, I need you to be really sure that's what you want."

"I've never been more sure of anything in my life. I want to make love with you, Sawyer."

Seeing the certainty that shone from her eyes, he gave in to the wild want that surged inside him. He kissed her again and this time when his hands caressed her back, they did so inside the soft cotton of her T-shirt.

She stopped the kiss, sat up and pulled her T-shirt off all in one fluid movement. With the faint glow of the fading sunshine sneaking through the slit in the draperies, she looked so beautiful she momentarily took his breath away.

"Now you," she said and plucked at his T-shirt.

He complied, taking it off and throwing it on the floor. When he kissed her again it was with her bare breasts against his chest. Her flesh was warm and her nipples were already erect, as if demanding immediate attention.

"Oh, woman, what you do to me," he said as he tore his mouth from hers.

He rolled with her in his arms so that he hovered over her and his mouth latched onto one of her turgid nipples. She clutched at his shoulders as a low, sexy moan escaped her.

He flicked his tongue over first one nipple and then the other, loving the taste of her and the sound of her pleasure. It didn't take long for the rest of their clothes to disappear.

Sawyer halted things only momentarily to pull the condom out of his wallet. He opened the package. When he was back in the bed, she took it from him and rolled it onto his hardness.

Things were going too fast, he thought. He wanted to explore every inch of her, to discover exactly what she liked and didn't like.

But it was too late. They were already past the point of exploration. He hovered between her thighs and stared down at her. Her lips were swollen and her cheeks were flushed. Her dark hair was a small halo around her head.

His love for her slammed into his chest, stealing his breath away even as he entered her. For a moment neither of them moved. He was lost in her warmth and it was only when she tightened her grip on his shoulders that he began to move his hips with hers.

Slowly at first and then faster… More frantic, they moved together. All too soon his climax was upon him, surging through him with an overwhelming force.

When it was finished, he held himself up on his elbows and looked down at her in dismay. "Uh… you didn't…"

"No, but it was still wonderful, Sawyer."

He rolled off of her, utterly disgusted with himself. "It was way too fast and I was selfish."

She laughed, a low, sexy sound. "Don't beat yourself up. There's always next time."

A new fire lit inside his stomach at the thought of making love to her again. He got off the bed and padded into the bathroom.

Minutes later he was back in the bed with her, both of them still naked. He pulled her into his arms and stroked the silky strands of her hair.

"I'll let you in on a little secret," she said.

"What's that?" he asked curiously.

"The after-glow is almost as good as an orgasm. And you're doing after-glow exceptionally well." She raised her head to smile at him and changed her position so that she lay across his chest with her head propped up on her crossed arms.

Instead of stroking her hair, he caressed her bare back. "I like to cuddle," he confessed.

"That's nice, because I like to cuddle, too," she replied. The smile on her face faded and her expres-

sion grew serious. "There's something I want you to
do for me, Sawyer."

"Anything," he replied easily.

"I want you to go home tonight and get a good
night's sleep. Then I want you to get back to your
routine and usual hours working on the ranch."

He stared at her for a long moment. "For real?"

"For real." She sat up and pulled the sheet up to
cover her bare breasts. "I feel safe here and Cassie
will never consider you for the foreman job if you
aren't there doing your work."

"But I want to be here with you...for you," he
protested. He sat up.

"And I know you're here for me," she replied. "Really, I'll be fine. You can come back here each night
after your dinner. The locks on the door are good
and I'm not going to open the door to just anyone."

The joy he'd been feeling a few minutes before
deflated out of him. Surely, if she cared about him
as much as he did her, she wouldn't be kicking him
out. Especially now, under the circumstances.

"But if I don't come back over until tomorrow
evening, what are you going to do for food all day
tomorrow?" He wasn't sure what he'd expected of
the night to come, but this wasn't it.

"I'll have Gary bring me over a burger at noon
and then, if you don't mind, maybe when you get
here we can go to the grocery store and I can pick
up a few things to tide me over until I leave here."

"Are you sure this is what you want?" he asked. He didn't like it. He would prefer to spend every waking and sleeping hour with her to make sure she stayed safe. But he couldn't force his will on her and he supposed she was as safe here as she could be as long as she didn't open the door to just anyone.

She hesitated a moment and then nodded. "I think it's what's best for both of us."

An hour later Sawyer was in his truck and headed for the ranch, but his heart was still in that motel room with her. He knew she was trying to do what was best for him in insisting that he do his daily work at the ranch, and that only deepened his feelings for her.

But it also made him question exactly what her feelings were for him. If she was in love with him, then wouldn't she have wanted him to stay through the night? Wouldn't she have wanted to sleep in his arms?

When he'd looked at her after making love with her, he'd seen his future. He'd seen himself sharing his life with her. He'd seen a house and babies and laughter. He'd seen morning coffee and a porch swing and the kind of love that would last a lifetime.

What hurt his heart was the possibility that when she looked at him she only saw an easygoing cowboy to see her through the darkness that had entered her life.

Chapter 9

Janis sat in the chair near the door in the motel room, waiting for Gary to bring her lunch. There were only three people she would open the door for: Gary, Dillon and Sawyer. Those were the only people she truly trusted at the moment.

Her thoughts had been filled with Sawyer since she'd opened her eyes that morning. Oh, how she'd wanted him to stay through the night. How she'd longed to sleep in his arms and awaken this morning to his lazy, sexy grin.

But the town would be buzzing with enough gossip without adding in Sawyer and Janis spending nights together at the motel.

She'd never spent the entire night with a man.

Maybe she was old-fashioned, but it had always felt wrong without a wedding ring on her finger. Funny that sleeping together seemed even more intimate than making love with a man.

She stood as Gary's van pulled up in the parking space right in front of her room. He got out, carrying a bag from the only drive-through burger joint in town.

She unlocked the door and he came inside, bringing with him the heady scent of hamburger and fries. "Thanks, Gary," she said as she took the bag from him and gestured for him to have a seat at the small, Formica-topped table.

"How are you doing?" he asked, dark concern on his blunt features.

"I'm okay right now," she replied, pulling the burger and fries out of the bag.

"I can't believe this happened in my establishment. I treat my employees well. I give my patrons good food and drinks at a reasonable price, but if it gets out that there are peepholes all over the place, my business could be ruined. And that doesn't even count the trauma you've been put through. God, Janis, I can't tell you how damned sorry I am."

She reached out and touched his beefy arm. "Gary, I'll be fine and your business will survive."

He released a deep sigh. "I would have liked to get Jesse to fill all those holes, but I guess Chief Bowie is right to leave them be and catch the pervert in action. Are you sure you're good with going back into the room?"

"Yeah, I'm thinking maybe I'll talk to Dillon about returning there day after tomorrow." She unwrapped her cheeseburger and took a bite despite the apprehension that swept through her.

She could go back there tonight and start the process to catch the creep, but she just felt like she needed a day or two to get up her nerve.

"And none of the men has ever appeared strange toward you?" he asked.

Janis shook her head and followed the bite of cheeseburger with a french fry. She knew Gary well enough to know he was on a rant and that when he was like this he mostly liked the sound of his own voice.

"I'll be interested to see what Chief Bowie learns today when everyone turns in their whereabouts for the afternoon Sawyer got shot. And if we don't find the bastard that way, then we'll see who's peeking in on you when you go back into the room." He banged his fist on the table, startling her to the point that she choked on a bite.

She coughed and reached for the glass of water she'd fixed herself while she'd waited for him. She took several deep gulps.

"Sorry, honey. I didn't mean to freak you out. This all just makes me so damned mad." He got up from the table. "I'll get out of here and let you finish eating in peace."

She got out of her chair and walked with him to the door. "Thanks for bringing me lunch," she said.

"It's the least I can do after everything you've gone through." He reached out and patted her on the back. "Hopefully it won't be long before we get this demented nutcase behind bars."

"From your lips to God's ears," she replied.

Half an hour later she sat on the bed and listened to the silence surrounding her. She wished Sawyer was with her. She wished he was telling her one of his funny stories and making her laugh. She wished for his calm nature to quiet the anxiety that filled her heart.

She usually didn't mind the silence, but today it pressed heavy and oppressive against her chest. Even thinking about time spent with her dad didn't bring her any relief.

She eyed the television but dismissed the idea of turning it on. She didn't need noise. What she needed was for Dillon to find the man who had her in his sights. It would be nice if he could find the man who'd shot Sawyer. She'd hoped that would happen before she had to go back to staying in the room. What she wanted was to be able to put this all behind her and get back to living her life to the fullest.

And she wanted to spend time with Sawyer and be able to go out without fearing that he'd be killed.

Just seeing the bandage on his shoulder last night had made her fear for his life.

Still, as her thoughts lingered on the night before, she couldn't help but smile. Making love with Sawyer had been magical. It had been intense and fiery and yet tender and perfect.

She'd loved the feel of his naked body against her, the smell of him that had lingered on her skin long after he'd left. She had no idea what the future might bring for the two of them. Right now she just intended to take things one day at a time.

There was no way she could think about a future when she felt a threat moving closer and closer every day.

By the time Sawyer arrived at just after six, she was positively sick of being in her own head and eager for his company.

The first thing they did was get into his truck for a trip to the grocery store. By the time they reached the store they had shared the events of their days with each other. He'd polished harnesses and saddles all day and she confessed she had finally resorted to watching game shows on television to pass the long afternoon.

She was ridiculously happy to see him and, at least for now, while in his company, all felt right with the world. "I made a grocery list so this shouldn't take long," she said when they entered the store.

He grabbed a basket as she pulled her list out of

her purse. "Take all the time you need. Do you like to cook?" he asked as they began walking down the produce aisle.

"I don't mind it," she replied. "Although with it just being me, I rarely go to the trouble of cooking a big meal. What about you?"

"I can do bacon and eggs and make a mean steak on the grill, but that's about it. With Cookie providing meals for all of us, learning how to cook has never been a big priority."

She grabbed salad fixings and placed them in the basket. As they wove their way up and down the aisles, they chatted about completely mundane things. It was exactly what she needed to calm the nerves that had flared up inside her since they'd found the peepholes.

Forty minutes later they were back in her motel room. She shooed him to sit at the table while she unloaded the bags. "I was hoping to hear from Dillon today," she said, placing sandwich meat in the refrigerator and then putting a bunch of bananas on the countertop.

"It's probably taking him all day to sort out the alibis that everyone was supposed to give him." He touched his shoulder.

"Have you looked at that since I bandaged it up?" she asked worriedly.

"Yeah. I changed the bandage this morning and rubbed on some more of the antibiotic cream. It's already starting to heal up, so get that worried look off your face."

"If I find the person who did that to you, I'll personally punch him in the nose as hard as I can," she said fervently. She slammed a package of chicken breasts down on the table to punctuate her point.

"Whoa, woman." He laughed. "I didn't know you had that kind of meanness in you."

"Ha, you hurt somebody I care about and watch how mean I can get," she replied.

"So, you care about me. That's nice to know." His eyes radiated that warmth that always shot straight into her heart and made her slightly giddy.

"Well, of course, I care about you, you big lug. If I didn't, then last night wouldn't have happened." A blush warmed her cheeks as she thought of their lovemaking.

"At least today I can actually talk about what happened last night instead of waking up in your bed and not remembering a darned thing."

She tried not to laugh but a giggle escaped her. "I'm sorry." She instantly attempted to sober. "Watching you dance around the conversation that morning was ridiculously amusing."

"It was horrifying," he replied, although his eyes twinkled with humor.

Sawyer had insisted she fix herself something to eat and she'd just finished a sandwich when a knock fell on the door.

Instantly, Sawyer was on his feet with his gun pulled. Her heart leaped into her throat. Sawyer's quick reaction was a stark reminder that nothing was normal in her life at the moment and danger could only be a door knock away.

Sawyer opened the door a mere inch and relaxed at the sight of Dillon standing outside. He holstered his gun and opened the door wider to allow the lawman inside.

"We were just wondering if we'd hear from you today," Sawyer said as the three of them sat at the table.

"Want a cup of coffee?" Janis asked. "I was just about to make a pot."

"Sure, I'd take a cup if you're making it." He swept a hand through his dark hair. "It's been a long day. I've been chasing down alibis for everyone from the bar for the day you were shot," he said to Sawyer.

"So, did everyone bring you a list of their activities for that day?" Janis asked as she poured water into the coffee machine.

"Everyone except Miguel and James. I've got a couple of men out looking for them now," Dillon replied.

"Have you checked out everyone else's alibi?" Sawyer asked, eager to find out if they were narrowing things down.

Dillon nodded. "Although there are a couple that

there is no way to substantiate. Charlie said he was at home alone and Rusty claims that he decided to go for a long drive since the weather was so nice."

Sawyer frowned. "Maybe he took a little drive to the ranch and parked in the woods and then shot me."

"Maybe," Dillon replied. "But at this point, I've got no evidence to arrest anyone. I'm in the process of digging deeper into those men's private lives."

"What about James and Miguel? Is it possible both of them are peepers and that's why they didn't bring you anything today?" The idea sickened Sawyer and he could only imagine how his question affected Janis.

"Right now anything is possible," Dillon replied. "But my gut is telling me this is one man who is obsessed with Janis. I think it's obvious his interest in her goes far beyond peeping, otherwise he wouldn't have left you that note and then shot you."

"Cream or sugar?" Janis's voice was slightly shaky as she asked Dillon. She set a cup of fresh brew in front of him.

"No, this is fine," he replied. He waited until she had served Sawyer and herself and was once again seated at the table.

"I still believe the only way to get this guy arrested is to catch him in the act," Dillon continued. "Have you thought about when you might want to return to the room?"

"Maybe day after tomorrow, if that's okay with

you?" Janis replied. Her fingers trembled as she wrapped them around her coffee cup.

Sawyer wanted to pull her into his arms and tell her she never had to go back there, but he couldn't. He agreed with Dillon that the only way this person would be caught was if she went back and Dillon caught him in the act.

"Whenever you're ready," Dillon replied. "I know how difficult it will be for you."

She gave a curt nod and took a sip of her coffee.

"So, what is the exact plan?" Sawyer asked.

"The only time this man can be peeping at Janis is when the bar is closed and I doubt that he's sitting there watching her all night while she sleeps. So, the optimal hours would be maybe an hour or so after the bar closes and then all day on Sunday."

"And you're going to be hiding in the bar during those hours?" Janis asked.

Dillon nodded. "I figure nobody will see me if I hide behind the bar since it's on the other side of the room from where the holes are located. From there I'll be able to hear if anyone comes in."

"You realize it's possible it might take several nights," Sawyer said. He reached out and took one of Janis's hands in his. Her fingers were icy cold and he hated like hell that she was going through this.

Even though it didn't appear to be a life-threatening situation for her, he couldn't imagine how horrible it would be to suddenly discover that somebody had been watching you in your most private moments. It was a violation of unimaginable proportions.

"I'm willing to do this for however long it takes," Dillon said, his dark eyes growing even darker. "This is my town and these kinds of things aren't welcome here."

"This shouldn't be welcomed anywhere," Sawyer replied, squeezing Janis's hand reassuringly.

"I stopped by the bar a little while ago and Gary had everything in the room covered with tarps and had set off a couple of bug bombs, to explain your disappearance. He'd also given everyone their keys back." Dillon took a drink of his coffee.

"I wonder how long those holes have been there," Janis said.

"There's no way to know," Dillon replied.

"Maybe they were already there when I first moved in. That was over ten years ago." Janis leaned forward slightly, a fragile hope lighting her eyes. "Maybe the person who made them doesn't even work at the bar anymore and nobody is peeping in on me."

Dillon frowned. "I wish we could go on that assumption, but we can't. That listening device wasn't ten years old. From what little I could tell about it, it was a relatively new model and it was active. Somebody was definitely listening to you, and that leads me to believe somebody has been watching you, as well."

The hope in her eyes faded away as she pulled her hand from Sawyer's and instead, once again, wrapped her fingers around her cup.

He wanted to grab her up and put her in his truck. To drive someplace far away from here where she didn't have to face this craziness, where the two of them could just be happy and in love.

"I'd better get out of here," Dillon said. He drained his coffee cup and stood. "I'll stay in touch and, Janis, I promise we're going to get this guy."

"Thanks, Dillon," she replied and stood to walk him to the door.

Once he was gone and the door was safely locked behind him, Sawyer pulled Janis into an embrace. She clung to him as he caressed his hand up and down her back, wanting to comfort her.

"I still can't believe this is all happening," she said into the crook of his neck.

"I know, but hopefully in the next couple of days we can put this all to bed and go on with our lives." He gave her an extra tight squeeze and then released her. "How about we cuddle on the bed and watch some mindless television?" he suggested.

"That sounds absolutely wonderful," she replied.

Minutes later, Sawyer was propped up with pillows on the bed and Janis cuddled against his side.

It took some channel-flipping before they decided to watch a sitcom that neither of them had seen before.

It was hard for him to concentrate on the shenanigans on screen with her so close to him. He didn't want to hear canned laughter. He wanted to hear hers. But at the moment he was fresh out of humorous stories to tell her.

Besides, he sensed that laughter wasn't what she needed at the moment. What she needed was his quiet support and the knowledge that he'd have her back no matter what. She needed the warmth of his body next to hers, hopefully giving her the strength to get through the next few days.

"The first thing I want to do when this is all over is take you out to the ranch and get you up on horseback," he said as a commercial played. "We'll enjoy a nice sunset ride and then have a picnic under the stars."

"That sounds perfect," she replied. "And we'll stop at the café so you can get a couple of pieces of that crème brûlée cake to take with us."

"Now that really sounds perfect," he replied.

He wanted to tell her that he was in love with her. Right now, with her body curled up next to him. The three words that held such power and the emotion behind those words trembled in his heart, on the tip of his tongue, but he swallowed them back.

Was he moving too fast? There was no question that things had developed quickly between the two of them. But each minute he spent with her only increased his certainty that she was the woman he wanted to be with for the rest of his life. He wanted her to give him babies. He wanted to have the kind of family he'd never had…with her.

But he was reluctant to share all this with her now, with the drama hanging over their heads. He didn't want anything to taint or to take away from his expression of his deep love for her. Now simply wasn't the right time.

The sitcom ended and another one began, and still they remained curled up together on the bed. She was so quiet and so relaxed against him he wondered if she'd fallen asleep.

But just when he was sure she was asleep, she raised her head to look at him. "I could have potentially put an end to all this tonight if I'd just gone back to the room."

He gently moved a strand of her hair away from her face. "Nobody expected you to go back there tonight. Besides, Dillon is still busy chasing down alibis and I imagine he needed some time to figure out his schedule in order to be in the bar during the nights."

"I can't wait until this is all over, but I don't ever want to live in that room in the bar again." She pulled herself up and sat cross-legged next to him.

"So, what are your plans?" he asked.

"I guess I'll talk to Mable Treadwell. She's got

that big house and is always looking for somebody to rent a room from her. Or I'll see what kind of house I can rent for a reasonable price."

She released a deep sigh. "If this had happened two or three years from now, I might have had the money to put down on my dream home. But, financially, I'm just not there yet."

"Tell me about this dream home of yours," he said, hoping the conversation would lighten the darkness in her eyes.

"I see it as a place here in town, probably a two-story with a big master suite and at least one or two guest rooms. I'd love it to have a wraparound front porch and a deck in the back."

Just as he'd hoped, her eyes shone with her dreams instead of shining with fear. "I've even kept a wish book filled with decorating ideas and color schemes." Her cheeks flushed with a blush. "I know it sounds crazy, but when I finally get my house, I want everything to be perfect. I want a place where I feel safe and happy and nobody can ever take it away from me or kick me out."

"That doesn't sound crazy at all." What he wanted to tell her was that he'd buy her that house, that he'd sit on the front porch and drink coffee with her in the mornings and watch the sunset from the back deck in the evenings. "And eventually those guest rooms could become children's bedrooms."

"Oh, I don't want any children," she said.

He stared at her in stunned surprise. She didn't want children? How could the woman of his dreams not want children when having babies was his dream?

Maybe she wasn't the woman of his dreams, after all.

Chapter 10

She could tell she'd shocked him, but this was something they hadn't talked about before. He stared at her with widened eyes.

"No kids, really?" he finally asked.

"No kids," she said firmly.

"Tell me about the issues you had with your mother," he said.

The sudden change of topic threw her off. Immediately old memories battered her and a new tension filled her body. "I really don't want to talk about that right now."

"Have you ever talked about it with anyone?" He replumped the pillows behind his head so he sat straighter.

"No," she admitted.

"Tell me, Janis." His eyes held a soft plea. "Maybe it would be good for you to talk about it."

She frowned thoughtfully. Would it be good for her to pierce the scab on the wounds her childhood had left behind by discussing it?

Could she talk about it with him? Tell him about all that pain? Maybe she'd just been waiting for him to come along. She certainly trusted him more than anyone else in her life.

Drawing in a deep breath, she began talking about the woman who had given her birth.

"I think my mother hated me from the minute I was born." She was shocked by the emotional tremble in her voice.

She coughed and then cleared her throat before continuing. "I don't have any memories of her giving me a kiss or hugging me or kissing me good-night when I was young. She was always cold and distant, but when I got older I realized just how much she hated me."

She got up from the bed, needing to move...to pace, while she delved into the darkness of her past.

"I learned quickly that when I got home from school the best place for me to be was in my bedroom, otherwise she'd find a reason to punish me."

"Did she physically abuse you?" Sawyer asked, his voice low and gruff.

"Not really, although sometimes she would pinch

me on my arms hard enough to leave a bruise. She mostly called me names and told me I was bad all the time. And then my dad would get home from work and tell me I was his princess and I was the best daughter anyone could have."

She paced the space between the bed and the kitchen table, her brain shooting her back in time. She could smell the scent of her mother's perfume, a heavy, spicy scent that brought no comfort to her.

June Little was a beautiful, vain woman who never stepped out of the house unless her makeup was perfect and her long, dark hair was neatly in place. She'd never offered to brush her daughter's hair or to do anything else for Janis.

"It wasn't until I was thirteen or fourteen that I realized the truth of the matter was that my mother was jealous of me." Her heart squeezed tight. "When my father bought me a new dress, she'd tell me I was fat and ugly and no new dress would ever fix that. When my father took me out someplace and spent time with me, my mother would tell me that I was a whiny bitch who forced him to do things with me."

"That's messed up," Sawyer said softly.

To her horror, tears burned at her eyes. She didn't want to cry…not about this. She had already shed a lifetime of tears over her relationship with her mother.

"Did you tell your father what she was doing, what she was saying to you?"

She shook her head. "My father was crazy about my mom. He positively adored her and I didn't want to put him in a terrible position between her and me. They had a wonderful marriage, but my mom looked at me as a competitor for his time and attention. She was so jealous of me and, in her eyes, I was the other woman trying to take him away from her."

The tears she'd tried so desperately to hold back slid down her cheeks. She wiped at them angrily. "When my father died, things got really bad. Not a day passed that she didn't tell me I was nothing but a whore who had stolen her precious time with him. For two years she battered me with hurtful words and told me over and over again that I was selfish and a wh-whore."

Sobs ripped through her. They were the cries of a little girl who had only wanted her mommy to love her and of grief over the man who had left her too soon.

Instantly, Sawyer was off the bed and gathering her into his arms. She leaned into him, drawing strength from his tight embrace even as she buried her face in the crook of his neck and cried the last of her tears.

"Shh," he whispered into her ear. "I wish you had had my mother."

A small laugh escaped her and she pulled away from him enough to look into his beautiful, handsome face. "And I wish you had had my father."

He used his thumbs to wipe her cheeks and smiled, a soft, wonderful smile that shot warmth straight to her heart. "Aren't we a pair," he said. "We're just a couple of orphaned puppies who somehow found each other."

He sobered and his eyes bore into hers intently.

"I'll tell you one thing, Janis, you are none of the things your mother told you that you were. I know who you are. I see into your heart and there's nothing there but goodness and kindness."

Oh, how she'd needed somebody to tell her that. His words were a welcomed balm to the sores she'd reopened in telling him about her childhood. She leaned her head into his chest and breathed in the scent of him.

A far different emotion welled up inside her. Need…want…desire for this man who was standing by her side and seemed to want to be there for as long as she needed, as long as she wanted him.

Once again she looked at him. "I'm so glad I had those cowboys put you in my bed."

"Me, too. Although now I don't need anyone to help me to your bed. I can get there under my own steam."

"Want to get there right now?"

She loved the way his eyes heated and held her gaze so intently. It was as if there was nothing else in the world except the two of them. She needed him now to take away the bad taste that talking about her mother had left behind.

"I'd love to," he replied before his mouth took hers in a kiss that spoke of tenderness and desire.

This time their lovemaking was slow and languid. He loved every inch of her body, teasing and tormenting her and bringing her again and again to the very brink. By the time it was all over, she'd climaxed twice and was wonderfully sated.

Afterward they remained in each other's arms. She lay across his chest and he softly stroked her hair. "You didn't finish your story. When you decided to leave home, did you and your mother have a big blow-out?"

"No, nothing like that. The day of my graduation from high school I packed some bags, got into my car and never looked back."

"So what did you do? Where did you go?"

"I stayed at friends' places and in my car. I applied for several jobs but found out my mother was telling people I was unreliable and a slut and not to hire me."

A lump rose in her throat as she remembered that time of such uncertainty. She'd fallen asleep each night scared and had awakened in the mornings with the same fear of what would become of her.

"Then one day I was sitting alone in the café having a cup of coffee when Gary asked if he could join me. We sat together and talked, and I confessed that I was not only looking for a job but also someplace to live. He offered to help me get a server license so he could hire me and the opportunity to live in the back room. I'm not sure what would have happened to me without his help."

"So, he was your Big Cass," Sawyer said. "I'm so glad he was there for you."

"Trust me, it was a good move for him, too. I'm on the property all the time to keep thieves away and I'm the best darned manager he's ever had," she said with a sense of pride.

"I don't doubt that for a minute," he agreed. He continued to stroke her hair. "Thank you for sharing with me, Janis. I know it wasn't easy for you to go back to that time in your life."

She sat up. "Thank you for listening. I think I needed to talk about it. I've held it all inside for a very long time."

"I hope shining a light on it helped chase away some of the darkness."

"It was definitely a time of darkness," she agreed.

He released a deep sigh. "I guess it's past time for me to get up and get out of here." He leaned over and kissed her on the forehead. "You don't have to get up."

He got out of bed, grabbed his clothes from the floor and padded into the bathroom. He was magnificent in his nakedness. Halena was right, he definitely had a great butt.

When he came back out of the bathroom he wore

his reluctance to leave on his features. "I'll give you a call tomorrow and check in with you and then I'll be back here around six or so."

She was torn, wanting him to stay with her through the night and yet feeling the need to be alone to untangle some of the emotion the night had brought.

"Okay, I'll talk to you tomorrow," she replied.

They said their good-nights and then, after he was gone, she pulled on her nightgown and walked over to the door to throw the dead bolt. She then crawled back into the bed. His scent was on her skin and lingered on the pillow.

She pulled the pillow against her chest as a new wave of tears burned hot and heavy behind her eyelids. She'd never considered herself a particularly emotional woman, but it seemed all she did right now was cry.

Her tears now were because she knew she was in love with Sawyer Quincy, and she was fairly certain he was in love with her. She should be deliriously happy, but she wasn't.

Tonight she'd realized that there was no way the two of them had a future together. He deserved a woman who had no crazy baggage, a woman who would give him lots of babies.

He'd be a wonderful father. There was no doubt in her mind that he would make each of his children feel loved and protected.

She could never be the right woman for him. There was no way that she wanted children she could screw up. She had no role model for mothering.

And she was selfish, like her mother had told her, because even knowing she wasn't right for Sawyer, she didn't want to let him go yet.

"You ever think about having kids?" Sawyer asked Clay the next morning. The two of them were in the tack room where Sawyer was cleaning and polishing equipment and Clay straddled a sawhorse, taking a break from mucking out stalls.

"Sure. Eventually, when I find the woman I want to spend the rest of my life with, I'd like a couple of rug rats. Why'd you ask?"

"You know I've always wanted kids," Sawyer replied.

Clay nodded. "You've talked about it often enough."

"What if you finally found the woman you wanted to spend the rest of your life with and discovered she doesn't want to have any kids?"

"Janis doesn't want to have kids?" Clay raised a blond eyebrow.

"That's what she says." Sawyer kind of understood it, given the relationship she'd had with her mother. But there was no doubt in his mind that Janis would be a wonderful, loving mother.

"Why? I'd think with all her practice mothering drunk cowboys she'd be a natural at it," Clay replied.

Sawyer laughed even though his heart was hurting. "She didn't have a good relationship with her mother and I'm pretty sure that's made her decide not to be a mother."

Clay tipped his black cowboy back on his head and gazed at Sawyer in speculation. "So, what does this do to your relationship with her?"

"Nothing right now. I just need to wrap my mind around a different kind of future for myself." He released a deep sigh.

"You're really into her, aren't you?" Clay asked.

Sawyer grinned at him. "I'm completely crazy about her," he admitted. "You all did me a big favor the night you put me in her bed."

"I can't believe you stopped drinking."

Sawyer leaned against the workbench. "I don't even miss it."

"I respect the decision you made to stop," Clay replied.

Sawyer looked at him in surprise. "Thanks, man. That means a lot."

Clay stood. "Guess it's time for me to get back to cleaning out horse crap. I'm glad we rotate positions so I don't have to do this every day."

"I imagine I'll be doing it tomorrow since you all won't let me do anything else but work here in the stables."

"None of us has forgotten that you still have a

target on your back and we aren't ready to bury you yet," Clay replied.

Sawyer laughed once again. "And I'm not ready to be buried yet."

"On that note, I'm back to work." Clay left the tack room, leaving Sawyer alone with his thoughts.

He hung the harness he'd just finished polishing and grabbed another dirty one, his thoughts full of the woman he loved.

Their lovemaking last night had been more than wonderful. When he was deep inside her, looking into her eyes, he felt as if he was finally home. When she curled up next to him or grabbed his hand or simply smiled at him, he got the same feeling.

She was where he belonged. The thought of not having kids was sad, but the thought of not having Janis in his life was too painful to bear.

He pulled his cell phone from his pocket, suddenly just wanting to hear the sound of her voice.

She answered immediately. "Hey, cowboy, aren't you supposed to be working?"

"I am working, I just had a sudden hankering to talk to my woman," he replied, unable to help the smile that not only stretched his mouth but also warmed his heart to the very core.

"Actually, I'm glad you called. I talked to Dillon a little while ago and told him I want to go back to the room tonight."

"Really? I thought you wanted a couple more days before going back," he replied in surprise.

"I just want it over, Sawyer." There was a deep weariness in her voice. "I'm ready to put the process into motion that will catch the person."

"I admire your strength, Janis," he said, his love for her buoying in his chest. "And I want this over for you. I'm just sorry you have to go through it in the first place. When this is all over, I'll help you find a place to live where you'll always feel safe."

"Will you come here after work and take me back to the bar?"

"Of course, and I'll stay there with you for as long as you want me to."

There was a long silence. "Janis, are you still there?"

"I'm here. I was just thinking that I can't imagine a better man than you, Sawyer. You deserve all the happiness in the world and all your dreams coming true."

There was a strange sadness in her voice that set him on edge. "They are," he replied. "Janis, you have to know that I love you." Geez, he hadn't intended to tell her over a phone call. How romantic was that?

There was another long pause. "I know. We'll talk later. I'll see you after work, right?"

"You know I'll be there." Before he knew it, she murmured goodbye and hung up.

Slowly he put his phone back in his pocket, drew

in a deep breath and then tipped his hat back on the top of his head as he straddled the sawhorse.

She hadn't said "I love you, too." He'd told her he loved her and she'd said they'd talk later. His heart thudded an anxious rhythm. What did that mean?

He'd come home last night and had lain awake for hours, sorting through the knowledge that, in binding his life with Janis's, he would achieve his dream of loving and being loved. But he would also have to say goodbye to the dream of having any children of his own.

Damn Janis's mother for taking the love of a little girl for her father and twisting it into something ugly and bad. Damn her for not loving her daughter the way a mother was supposed to. Didn't people realize how sensitive, how vulnerable, children were? Didn't her mother know a single unkind word would cut like a knife?

Could he build a life with Janis without children? The answer he'd reached at some point over the last hour was an overwhelming yes. He wasn't willing to give her up for any reason.

Having her as a wife, as a friend and lover for the rest of his life was everything he'd ever wanted for himself. But she hadn't said "I love you, too."

With another heavy sigh, he stood, knocked his hat into place and went back to work. Yes, they were going to talk tonight and he hoped he could convince her that he was her dream for a future of happily-ever-after.

As usual, at five o'clock the men began their walk through the buffet line in the cowboy dining room. The scent of barbecued beef and beans rode the air, making Sawyer's mouth water. There was nothing better than Cookie's barbecue.

Sawyer was quiet throughout the meal, consumed by thoughts of the night to come. Would the peeper be so eager to watch Janis again that he'd make an appearance tonight and Dillon would finally get him behind bars? Or would it take days or even weeks before that happened?

He absolutely hated the very idea of Janis having to stay in a place where she felt unsafe and violated. Unfortunately he agreed with Dillon that this was the only way to catch the creep.

We'll talk later. He'd told her he loved her and she'd said they would talk later. There was no way she could convince him that she didn't care deeply about him. He didn't believe she was the kind of woman who could make love to him so passionately if she wasn't in love with him.

So what did she want to talk about? The question thrummed through him as he showered and dressed. It rode with him in his truck as he headed to the motel.

Nerves jangled inside him, something he wasn't accustomed to. Before Janis, he hadn't had a worry in the world. Now he worried for her and about her. He was concerned about how the night might play out.

They already knew the peeper had a gun and wasn't afraid to use it. If Dillon confronted him in the darkness of the bar, would the perp pull out the gun and shoot? And then what?

His shoulder suddenly ached, as if his worry had coalesced into making the wound he'd received re-open. Maybe Dillon had already planned for just such an event. Perhaps he had another officer who would be in the bar with him when the bar went dark for the night.

He pulled up in front of her motel room and, even with everything that was on his mind, his spirits lifted in anticipation of seeing her again.

Getting out of the truck he could only hope that this all ended tonight and that he and Janis could get on with the rest of their lives.

He knocked on the door and waited, but there was no answer. With a frown, he knocked again, this time harder. Still there was no reply.

A dreadful disquiet swept through him. He banged a third time on the door. Maybe she was in the shower, he thought. He immediately dismissed the idea. She knew about what time he would be ar-riving to pick her up; she wouldn't have planned a shower at the same time.

So why wasn't she answering? The disquiet grew

inside his chest, pressing tightly and making it difficult for him to breathe.

He called her phone. It rang four times and then went to her voice mail. He called again with the same result. "Janis, give me a call the minute you get this message," he said and then hung up.

Stay calm, he told himself. Maybe Dillon had already come to get her and she hadn't had a chance to tell Sawyer about the change in plans.

Once again he pulled his cell phone out of his back pocket and punched in the number to connect him to the chief of police. He answered on the second ring.

"Dillon, is Janis with you?" he asked without preamble.

"No. I'm at home. I thought you were taking her back to the bar this evening."

"I was supposed to, but I'm here at the motel and she isn't answering the door." The anxiety that had bubbled in his chest exploded into a full-blown fear.

"Sawyer, don't do anything. Don't even try to enter that room. I'll be over there as soon as I can." With that said, Dillon hung up.

Once again Sawyer banged on the door, even though he knew if she was inside she would have already answered. She wasn't in there.

The earth felt dangerously shaky beneath his boots as he walked back to his truck and sat, his cell phone in his hand. Gary. Maybe Gary had taken her back to the bar.

Even though he knew he was reaching, he called the bar owner. "Sawyer, what's up?"

"Where are you?" Sawyer asked.

"I'm at the bar. I just finished pulling all the tarps out of Janis's room so it's ready for her. I even bought a little bouquet of flowers that will hopefully cheer her up."

"So, she isn't with you?"

"No. I haven't seen or spoken to her since I took her lunch yesterday."

The bottom of Sawyer's stomach plummeted to the ground. "Thanks, Gary."

Where was Dillon? They needed to get inside her room as quickly as possible. Maybe she'd fallen and hit her head and was lying on the floor unconscious.

Again he got out of his truck, unable to sit still while he waited. He could at least go ahead to the motel office and get the room key. That way, when Dillon did arrive, they could go right in.

He hurried down the sidewalk to the motel office, his heart racing with a simmering panic he refused to give in to.

Fred sat in a chair behind the desk, reading a tabloid.

"Fred, I need a key to room seven," he said.

He watched impatiently as Fred carefully folded the paper, set it aside and then stood. "That room is rented to Janis."

"I know that. Could I have the key?"

Fred frowned. "I'm not in the habit of just handing out keys willy-nilly. I only give them to the person who has rented the room."

Sawyer fought the impulse to jump over the counter. "Fred, I think Janis is in some kind of trouble. Chief Bowie is on his way over and we need the key to get inside, unless you want me to break down the door."

At that moment Dillon's car pulled up in front of the building. "Will you give me the key now?" Sawyer asked in frustration.

"I'll give it to the chief," Fred said with a self-righteous tone that made Sawyer want to punch the man in his oversize nose.

"Do you have the key?" Dillon asked Sawyer when he entered the office.

"I have it right here," Fred said and passed the key across the counter toward Dillon.

Sawyer snatched it up and headed for the door, certain that Dillon was right on his heels.

"I talked to her earlier today and we made plans for me to pick her up and take her back to her room in the bar when I got done with work," he said.

They reached her unit and Sawyer's fingers shook as he inserted the key into the lock.

"Janis?" he shouted as the two men stepped into the room.

Her purse was on the table and her suitcase stood by the door as if ready to go.

Sawyer stalked to the bathroom. The door was open and she wasn't there. She was nowhere in the room.

She was gone…but where?

Chapter 11

Janis struggled for consciousness against the darkness that filled her head. It would be so easy to fall back into that numb, dark place, but a sense of urgency beat through her veins, telling her she needed to wake up.

Where was she? A rhythmic sound and motion told her she was in a vehicle. How had she gotten there? And where was she going? It somehow just didn't matter right now.

She was so sleepy, simply opening her eyelids felt like too hard a task. The darkness reached out and, with a soft sigh, she plunged into it and knew no more.

The next time a vague consciousness came to her,

she knew she was no longer in a vehicle. The sound and the motion were gone and she was surrounded by stillness and silence.

So where was she? Damn the grogginess that battled her wits. She stretched out her legs and realized she was in a bed. Had she decided to take a nap? Had she only dreamed about being in a vehicle?

Wasn't it about time for Sawyer to come to get her? Tonight they would hopefully catch the man who was obsessed with her. But first she needed to wake up. Why did she feel so…so drugged?

She drew in several deep breaths and released each one slowly, hoping to clear her head. Finally she cracked open her eyes. She was in a bed, but it wasn't the motel room bed.

It was a double-size bed dressed in pale lavender sheets. There was a dark purple spread covering her. Her heart began to beat more quickly. Not her bed. It wasn't her bed in the motel room and it wasn't her bed in the back of the bar.

She slowly sat up, a wealth of horror overwhelming her as she looked around. She was in a large room. There was not only the bed and a nightstand, but also a sitting area with a recliner chair and a coffee table.

There was a fully equipped kitchen and a kitchen table and chairs. Next to the refrigerator was a stacked washer and dryer.

But none of those things caused her heart to nearly stop beating and bile to rise in the back of her throat.

The whole room appeared to be a studio apartment, with everything a person would need to live comfortably. However, the entire area was surrounded by a glass enclosure. And the glass enclosure appeared to be in the middle of a building.

She was in an oversize fish tank without fish, a terrarium without frogs or lizards. She was the live species within the glass.

She jumped off the bed, but had to sit back down as a wave of dizziness overtook her. Dear God, how had she gotten here? Who? Who had brought her here? And where exactly was here?

She squeezed her eyes tightly closed to shut out the sight of her surroundings. Fought against the panic and terror, and instead tried desperately to think.

She'd been in the motel room watching television as she'd waited for the time when Sawyer would come to get her. She'd just eaten a sandwich for lunch and had turned on the television to pass the time. She remembered the game show that had been playing and the little gray-haired woman that everyone in the audience had been cheering for.

Somebody had knocked on her door. Who had it been? Who? Her mind remained blank. Why could she remember eating a ham-and-cheese sandwich and the gray-haired woman on the television and yet couldn't remember who had been at her door?

Why didn't she know who had brought her to this nightmare? And it was definitely something out of a nightmare. As the full realization of her situation struck her, her heart nearly beat out of her chest.

She had to get out. She had to figure out a way to escape. Right now, on the other side of the glass enclosure, she didn't sense anyone in the darkness of the surrounding building. Once again she pulled herself to her feet. She walked on shaky legs across the room and to the glass.

She touched it with her fingers, as if needing to confirm to herself that it was really there. It felt slightly cool to her fingertips. She dropped her hand to her side and backed away.

This was like something out of a sci-fi movie where aliens had placed her under a glass dome to study her. Only it wasn't the action of an alien. It was a man she knew, a man she worked with, and he had gone to enormous extremes to make sure he possessed her.

A scream begged to be released but she swallowed it down. Screaming wouldn't help her now. Tears burned at her eyes, but she refused to allow them to fall. She needed to keep her head about her and to find a way out.

She walked to the kitchen table and grabbed one of the iron chairs. She carried it to the closest wall of the enclosure. With all her might, she threw it at the glass.

The chair bounced back without doing any damage to the glass. So it was some kind of strong Plexiglas and there was no way out through it.

She wandered around, seeking some hope of escape, but her horror continued to grow. Even the bathroom area was out in the open. There was only one place to hide in the entire structure and that was a wooden pantry in one corner of the kitchen area.

Still, as she looked at all the food in the refrigerator, as she stared at all the items in the fully stocked pantry, she realized there were enough supplies to keep somebody in here for a very long time.

It was then that the scream she'd been holding back released.

"Where is she, Dillon?" Sawyer stood in the middle of the motel room with Janis's scent surrounding him and the taste of fear in his mouth.

"I don't know. There's no sign of a struggle," Dillon said slowly.

"But her purse is here. She wouldn't have gone off somewhere without her purse and her phone. She's in trouble, Dillon. We have to find her."

"Why don't you head over to the bar to see if she might already be there," Dillon replied. "Maybe she had a friend pick her up. Meanwhile, I'll get a few of

my men over here to canvass the area to see if anyone saw her leave."

As he drove the short distance to the bar, Sawyer
prayed she would be there. But he knew there was
no way a friend had picked her up from the motel
room. There was no way Janis would have gone off
without her purse containing her cell phone.

He thought about the conversation they'd shared
earlier. Was it possible he'd freaked her out by telling her he was in love with her?

Had she run someplace to get away from him?
No, she hadn't run anywhere, not without her purse
and her suitcase. His heart, his very soul, told him
she was in deep trouble. Whoever had been peeping into her room had taken her and now had her all
to himself.

He pulled his phone out and dialed Clay's number. Clay answered on the first ring. "Janis is missing. Meet me at the bar," he said.

"Got it," Clay said and hung up.

Sawyer clutched the steering wheel tightly, his
heart pounding a frantic beat it had never known before. *Janis... Janis*, his heart cried out. Where could
she be? Who had taken her away from him?

The minute he'd seen her purse on the table, he'd
known that foul play was involved. The only thing
he could hope for was that the man who had taken
her didn't want her dead, he just wanted her all to
himself.

But who was it? Who had her and where had he taken her? He tried to shove away his emotions in an effort to stay clearheaded, but fear clawed inside him like a wild, trapped animal.

He reached the bar and stalked inside, his gaze shooting around the room. How he wanted to see her in her Watering Hole T-shirt and tight jeans, with a serving tray in her hand. How he wished her bright, loving smile greeted him.

Gary was sitting in a corner booth with several other men, a pitcher of beer in front of him. He got up the minute he saw Sawyer. "Did you find her?" he asked.

"She isn't here?" Sawyer asked even though he knew the answer.

"No. The room is all ready for her, but she hasn't been here. Her car is still parked out back."

"I want to see her room for myself." Sawyer went to the door that led to the room Janis had called home. It took only a glance to know that nobody was inside.

He turned on his heels and spied Annie across the room. He knew Annie and Janis were good friends. Was it possible Annie knew something? He wove his way through the tables to where the young woman stood taking orders from a group of four.

"Excuse me," he said to the people at the table. "Annie, have you heard from Janis today?"

Annie frowned. "No, why?"

"She's gone missing." The words ripped at his insides and tears burned hot at his eyes. He sucked them back. Now wasn't the time to be weak.

He had to be strong…stronger than he'd ever been before in his life. Damn it, he had to find the woman he loved.

"Oh, my God, what can I do?" Annie asked.

"Right now, nothing. But if you hear from her, let me know immediately." Sawyer turned on his heels, not wanting to waste any more time talking to somebody who probably wouldn't be of any help.

He headed back toward Gary, but before he got there, the door opened and the men from the Holiday Ranch walked in. A large lump formed in Sawyer's throat at the sight of Clay, Mac, Flint and Jerod. Following behind them he saw Tony, Brody and Dusty.

These were seven of the men he'd grown up with, men he considered his brothers, and he'd never been as happy to see them as he was at this minute. They'd always had each other's back and if one of them was in trouble the others helped. He definitely needed their help now.

"What can we do?" Clay asked as Gary stepped up to Sawyer's side.

Before he could reply, Cassie flew in the door. "Dillon told me about Janis. If it's okay with Gary, we'll make this our base camp until she's found."

"Whatever you need, I'm in," Gary replied.

"Right now what we need to do is check out

everyone who works here," Sawyer said, his brain working overtime. Tanner was working behind the bar so he wasn't a suspect. "Who's working in the kitchen right now?"

"Charlie and Denny," Gary replied.

"Denny?" Sawyer didn't know anyone named Denny who worked in the kitchen.

"Denny Grange. He's a new hire. Charlie is training him."

Sawyer's brain continued to assess what needed to be done. "Clay, see if you can run down Rusty Bratton. Flint, I want you to check out Miguel Gomez."

He continued to assign men to check on anyone who worked at the bar but wasn't working in the place at the moment. "Tony, I'd like you to check on Myles Hennessy and, Flint…same with Damon West." The flirt and the widower weren't really suspects, but Sawyer didn't want to leave anything to chance. "All of you check back in here as soon as possible," he finished.

As everyone ran to the exit, a hollow wind blew through Sawyer. Where was she? Who had taken her away and where was she now?

He wanted to run outside and go to each and every house in the area. He needed to tear open doors and search all the rooms in Bitterroot. He needed to scream her name at the top of his lungs.

But he also knew the smartest thing he could do at

the moment was to wait for reports to come in. Somebody had to be in charge here until Dillon arrived.

He sank down at a table and lowered his head as his heart continued to cry out. They should have taken everything much more seriously than they had. And yet, when he looked back, he wasn't sure what he would have changed or done differently.

"I've made two big pots of coffee."

Cassie's voice pulled him from his thoughts. He looked up to see her with two cups of coffee in her hands. She slid one of the cups in front of him and then joined him at the table.

"We've got to find her, Cassie," he said.

"We will," she replied firmly. "You've already set in motion a search team and Dillon is working the neighborhood around the motel. Hopefully somebody will either come back with her or with answers as to where she might be."

"I want to be out there searching for her, but I feel like my place is here right now."

She covered one of his hands with hers, her blue eyes gazing at him earnestly. "Sawyer, you've got the best men out looking for her right now. You know the cowboys will do anything in their power to bring her home to you." She pulled her hand back.

"I know." He wrapped his cold fingers around the coffee mug. "I love her, Cassie. I love her like I've never loved anyone before in my life."

"I'm happy for you, Sawyer, and we're all determined to find her."

He nodded and turned his gaze toward the door.

Dusk had fallen and, all too soon, night would arrive. He couldn't imagine the darkness of night falling without her. He wished he could somehow hold back the night until she was safe and sound in his arms once again.

It didn't take long before everyone who had come to the bar for an evening of fun and drinking discovered one of their favorite waitresses was missing.

Sawyer hadn't realized just how many friends he'd made over his years in Bitterroot, and Janis had just as many. Familiar faces appeared, asking what they could do to help.

Gary cut the menu items and drinks to half price and, while Sawyer appreciated everyone who was showing up to help, the only person he wanted to see was Janis or, at the very least, one of his cowboys coming back with vital information.

Tony was the first one back. "Myles was at home. He invited me inside and appeared genuinely horrified when I told him Janis was missing. Sorry, Sawyer, but I don't think he's your man."

Sawyer nodded. He hadn't really believed it was somebody who didn't work at the bar. Myles had been a long shot.

"I'm going to drive around and ask questions and see what I can find out," Tony said.

"Thanks," Sawyer replied. "I'm going to just step outside to get a breath of fresh air."

He followed Tony outside and watched as he got into his truck and pulled away.

Night had arrived and the darkness threatened to seep into Sawyer's heart and consume him.

He told himself it was far too early to lose hope, but nobody knew exactly what time she had gone missing.

Had she been kidnapped an hour before Sawyer had arrived at her motel room? Or had somebody taken her minutes after he'd spoken to her that morning?

Drawing in a deep breath of fresh air, once again tears burned hot at his eyes. He didn't care if she loved him or not. All he wanted was for her to be safe and sound.

The tears burned hotter and hotter and a sob escaped him. Was she dead? Had she been murdered by the man who wanted her all to himself? Would the sick bastard decide that by killing her he could somehow possess her forever?

Oh, God, the tears trekked down his cheeks at the dark thoughts. He walked to the side of the building and hunched over, unsure if he was going to choke on the tears or throw up.

He'd let her down. He'd promised he'd keep her safe, but he'd failed her. Damn it, he should have insisted he stay with her at the motel. He should have never left her there alone for even a minute.

He didn't know how long he'd been quietly weeping when Dillon's car pulled up.

Sawyer wiped the tears from his cheeks and drew in a deep breath. These were the only moments of weakness he would allow himself, he thought. He had to stay strong. He had to stay in control to see this through.

"You got anything for me?" he asked Dillon as he came around the corner of the building.

In the light spilling out of the bar window he saw Dillon grimace. "We canvassed the area around the motel and asked questions to see if anyone saw a vehicle parked at the motel or Janis being taken out of the room."

"Let me guess, nobody saw anything."

"Right," Dillon said. "Cassie told me you were handling a search effort from here."

"I've got men out hunting down anyone who is an employee here but isn't at work tonight," Sawyer replied.

Dillon clapped him on the back. "Let's go inside and you can fill me in."

Minutes later the two men were seated at a table. Cassie brought Dillon a cup of coffee and refilled Sawyer's cup, and then stood like a blond-haired sentry keeping others away from their table so the two of them could talk alone.

Sawyer told him which cowboy he had sent to check on who and that he was just waiting for the men to check in. "I couldn't have taken care of things here better myself," Dillon said. "I've got all my men driving the streets. I mean, maybe she wasn't taken from that room. Maybe she hit her head and is wandering the streets and suffering from some sort of amnesia."

"Do you really believe that?" Sawyer asked dryly.

Dillon drew in a deep breath. "No. Let's hope one of those cowboys of ours returns with something for us."

Within an hour most of them had returned. Rusty Bratton was at home playing video games with a friend. Widower Damon West had also been at home and in bed alone. Everyone was where they were expected to be except James, the maintenance man, and Miguel, the cook. There was no sign of either of the men.

Dillon called two of his officers and told them to sit on the houses belonging to the men.

"James was in here to clean last night, but I haven't heard from Miguel since we had the staff meeting," Gary said. "But then, he wasn't on the schedule to work."

"If either of those men has harmed a hair on her head, I'll kill them," Sawyer said with dark menace.

"They have to go home sooner or later and, when

they do, they'll have a lot of questions to answer," Dillon said.

"And in the meantime?" Sawyer asked.

"In the meantime we keep men out on the streets pounding the pavement and asking questions. That's all we can do right now."

The minutes ticked by in agonizing slowness. Sawyer paced... He prayed and felt his hope attempt to drift away.

At midnight the bar closed for business but remained open as the point of contact for anything relating to Janis's disappearance.

"I'm leaving the bar keys with Dillon," Gary said when it was almost one in the morning. "I've got to go home and get some sleep."

Everyone who left the place looked like they needed sleep. Despite the fear that had been an unrelenting companion to Sawyer, even he felt exhaustion tugging at him.

"Sawyer, why don't you head on home?" Dillon suggested. "I'll call you if anything breaks here."

"No way. I'm not leaving here until she's found," he replied. "I'll go back in her room and stretch out for a little while."

Wearily, he rose from the table and headed for the room Janis had called home. Gary's little bouquet of flowers sat on the nightstand. It was a bunch of daisies in an oversize smiley-face cup.

God, he was such a mess, he even resented the

happy face on the small vase. He moved it across the room next to the coffeemaker and then stretched out on the bed.

Instantly he was overwhelmed by grief. The scent of her was still in the sheets and he imagined he could feel the heat from her body.

She had to still be alive. She just had to be. He wasn't even close to being ready to tell her goodbye.

He closed his eyes, but he knew sleep wouldn't come. His mind was too busy working everything over, seeking clues or possibilities that might have been overlooked, anything that could bring her home.

He rolled over and stared at the wall where he knew the peepholes were located. "I'm going to find you, you bastard," he said aloud. "I'm going to find you and then I'm going to kill you."

Sawyer awakened at just after five in the morning. He hadn't slept but an hour or so and he absolutely hated himself for nodding off at all.

He left Janis's bedroom and went into the kitchen to make coffee. Dillon was still in the bar, slumped back in a booth and asleep.

Sawyer stood at the coffee machine, watching the dark brew drip into the carafe. She'd been gone all night. Nobody had seen anything. Nobody had heard anything. She'd been gone all night and they didn't know where to begin to look for her.

He'd fallen asleep with the taste of fear in his

mouth, and it was still there, just as strong and acrid as ever. The horror that she was gone still resonated deep inside him.

What wasn't as strong as it had been in the initial hours following her kidnapping was hope. Although it was still a faint glimmer deep in his heart, it had lost the full flame of complete confidence.

He poured himself a cup of coffee then turned and nearly jumped out of his skin. Dillon stood in the doorway. "Geez, man. You scared the hell out of me," he said.

"Sorry, I smelled the coffee."

"Do you smell my pain? My fear?" Sawyer asked and then grimaced. "Sorry, I know you're on my side."

"It's all right. I'm surprised you haven't completely exploded by now." He moved to the coffeepot and poured himself a cup.

"I'm normally not the exploding kind, but if anything will make me become that kind of man, it's this. James didn't come in last night?"

"No, he's still on the MIA list, but Miguel snuck in around two. He confessed he's in the country illegally and didn't want to get involved in any investigation of any kind. But the last thing he wanted was for us to believe he's responsible for whatever happened to Janis. He told me he'd rather be deported than have this town believe that of him."

"He's been a resident of Bitterroot for a long time.

Are you going to turn him in to the appropriate authorities?"

Dillon frowned. "Right now Miguel's status is the last of my concerns. As soon as we get some men rounded up, I want an all-out assault on this town to find James. He's the only person who works here that we haven't been able to check his alibis."

"And it's damned suspicious that he's gone missing at the same time as Janis."

"Exactly." Dillon motioned for the two of them to leave the kitchen. They settled back in the booth where Dillon had been snoozing.

"I've got a team of my officers coming in at six, but I'll be honest with you, the extra help from the men from the ranch doesn't hurt."

"I can have them back here with a single phone call," Sawyer replied. "What do we know about James?"

"He's fifty-seven years old. He's been divorced for the past ten years and lives in a small ranch house on Oak Street. According to his neighbors, he hasn't been home for a couple of days, but they also say that isn't particularly unusual for him. A couple of times a month he isn't at home for a few days."

"So where does he go when he isn't at home?" A gnaw of urgency was once again in the pit of Sawyer's stomach.

"Nobody knows."

"How positive are we that he's not in the house?

Can't you make a case for a search warrant?" Sawyer leaned forward. "She could be in that house right now, Dillon, while we're sitting here drinking our coffee." The very idea was torturous for Sawyer.

Dillon frowned once again. "We don't have any concrete evidence to tie him to anything and she hasn't even been missing for twenty-four hours yet, but maybe I can make a case to Judge Dickenson to get a warrant on circumstantial evidence."

"Then do it, man," Sawyer exclaimed.

Forty-five minutes later Dillon had a search warrant in hand and he and Officer Ben Taylor were ready to leave to execute it.

"Don't even think you're going over there without me," Sawyer said fervently. "I can either ride with you or get there under my own steam, but I will be there when you get inside."

Dillon frowned. "Okay, you can come with us, but I don't want you getting in our way or firing your gun for any reason."

"Got it," Sawyer replied but he didn't make a promise. If James had Janis someplace in his house and he'd hurt her, then all bets were off as to whether Sawyer would fire his gun or not.

He got into the back of Dillon's car, a wave of anticipation rushing through him. The sun was just coming up in the eastern sky, splashing ribbons of pink and orange across the horizon.

They should have done this last night, he thought

as Dillon backed out of the parking space in front of the bar. They should have stormed James's home in the dark of night. But he doubted that Dillon would have been able to get a search warrant then. It had been too soon.

The last thing Sawyer wanted was anything a defense lawyer could use to keep the perp out of jail. Everything had to be done by the book to assure not only an arrest but also a conviction.

Now Sawyer couldn't wait to get to the house. He prayed that Janis was there, unharmed but a prisoner. He wanted to rescue her and hold her in his arms. He wanted to smell the scent of her hair, feel the warmth of her body next to his. He ached with his need of her.

Nobody spoke as they drove the couple of blocks to the house on Oak Street. Sawyer leaned forward, straining against his seat belt as if that somehow could make them arrive faster.

He was out of the car at the house before Dillon had turned off the engine. As he waited for Dillon and Ben to get out of the car, he stared at the house.

It was a small ranch, painted dull beige, with dark green shutters. There were no lights on to indicate anyone was at home, but it was still early. It was quite possible James was a late sleeper since he worked in the wee hours of the night at the bar. But he hadn't showed up for work last night.

Sawyer was just behind Dillon when he approached the front door. Ben had gone around to the back of the house to make sure nobody exited that way. Dillon knocked. Firm, loud knocks that would raise the dead. "James, it's Chief Bowie. Open the door," he shouted.

No reply. He knocked again and still nobody answered the door. "Stand back," he said.

Sawyer took a step back and Dillon kicked the door. Once…twice…and, on the third time, it popped open with a crack of broken wood.

Dillon drew his gun, as did Sawyer, and together they entered into a small foyer. Sawyer's heart pounded in his chest as they walked into the living room.

The room was neat and clean with a dark brown sofa and matching recliner. There was a television mounted on the wall above a short bookshelf.

In the kitchen everything appeared to be in order. In the dish drainer next to the sink was one dinner plate and one glass. Still Sawyer's nerves jangled and his heart was in his throat as they moved down the hallway where all of the doors in the three-bedroom house were closed.

He held his gun steady as Dillon opened the first door and swept inside. A whoosh of disappointment left him as he saw a neatly made bed and a dresser. It was obviously a guest room and there was no sign that Janis had ever been there.

When they had checked every single room and

every closet or hiding place, a bitter disappointment welled up inside Sawyer. It was a disappointment so great he wanted to weep.

James had been their biggest suspect. If he wasn't guilty, then who?

"Does he own any other property?" he asked Dillon as they drove back to the bar.

"Not that I'm aware of," Dillon replied. "But I'd have to check with Suzie Anderson." Suzie had become city clerk a month before. Sawyer didn't personally know her but he desperately hoped she could help them.

When they returned to the bar, Dillon called Suzie and asked for any information she could give them concerning James owning any other property in town. She promised to get back to them as soon as she could.

By seven o'clock, not only were there patrolmen out looking for James, but also several of the Holiday Ranch cowboys had returned to help in the search.

Once again Sawyer found himself in a torturous waiting game that made him want to scream in frustration. It was just after nine when Suzie called Dillon to tell him there was nothing on file that indicated James owned any other property but the house where he lived.

"We need to be checking all the empty barns and vacant houses in the area," Sawyer said to Dillon. The idea of Janis tied up and lying on a bed of moldy old hay filled his head. He shook his head to dispel the horrifying vision.

"I've already got men doing that," Dillon replied. "We're all doing whatever we can, Sawyer."

"I know," he replied. "I'm going to step outside for a few minutes." He got up from the booth and headed to Janis's room, deciding he'd stand just outside her door.

He needed to escape the bar's interior for a few minutes. It had begun to feel like utter hopelessness inside those walls. He stepped outside and saw somebody run around the side of the building.

What the hell? Who would be out there skulking around? Adrenaline spiked through him as he took off running. He turned the corner and saw James.

Sawyer grabbed him by the collar of his shirt and slammed him up against the side of the building.

"Where is she?" Sawyer had his face so close to James's he could see the large pores in the man's nose.

"I don't know. I didn't have anything to do with her disappearance," James said frantically.

"What are you doing hiding out back here?" Sawyer wanted to bash his head into the wall. He needed James to be guilty. Damn it, he desperately wanted to believe that James could tell him where Janis was.

"I was hoping to catch Dillon all alone." James struggled to escape Sawyer's tight grasp on his shirt, but Sawyer held on tight.

"Where in the hell have you been?" Sawyer asked, his frustrated anger and fear peaking.

"Let me go. I need to talk to Dillon," James said angrily.

"Then let's go." Sawyer released his shirt and instead grabbed him by the arm and marched the man through Janis's room and into the bar where Dillon was seated in the booth.

"Look who I found lurking around the back door," Sawyer said as he shoved James in front of Dillon.

Dillon stood, his eyes narrowed. "Where have you been the last two days, James?"

James cast a glance toward Sawyer. "I kind of wanted to talk to you alone about that."

"You can talk to me now," Dillon said. "What do you know about Janis's disappearance?"

"Nothing… I don't know anything about what happened to her," James exclaimed.

"Then where in the hell have you been?" Sawyer asked.

"With Ivy Martin." James's cheek flushed red.

"Ivy Martin?" Dillon stared at the man.

"Yeah…you know her husband…he travels a lot and…" James's voice trailed off.

"You two are having an affair," Sawyer said flatly.

James gave a curt nod of his head. "I just didn't want it getting out. She's a nice lady and she doesn't want problems in her marriage."

Sawyer fought back a hysterical burst of laughter. While they had been desperately hunting for the man, assuming he was behind Janis's kidnapping, James's biggest crime was bedding a married lady.

So, who had Janis?

Chapter 12

There was no escape.

Janis had come to that conclusion after hours of exploring her glass prison. As her head cleared and after the initial horror had passed, she began to build a wall around the bathroom area. The kitchen table was turned on its side to form one wall, and she covered the chairs with sheets she'd found in the pantry and built a wall on the other side.

She still didn't remember how she had gotten here or who had brought her to this horrific place that appeared to have been built specifically for her.

The freezer was stocked with plenty of bags of french fries and her favorite canned goods were in the pantry. The bedding was all in shades of purple and pink, her favorite colors. Even the toilet paper was the same brand as what she used at home. It was all so creepy…so sinister.

She had no idea whether it was day or night. There were no clocks on the wall and no windows. She had no way to tell what time it was. She didn't know how long she'd been here, but it felt like an eternity. She couldn't even find a light switch to turn the overhead lights off and on.

Although she was tired, she didn't want to sleep. Not here where somebody could creep in on the other side of the glass and watch her.

What kind of a person did this? Who did she know who was messed up enough and had the resources to build something like this? This had taken months of preparation, of building and plotting and planning. And that was horrifying in and of itself.

She now sat on the edge of the bed, waiting for something to happen, for somebody to come in. Her heart pounded a frantic rhythm that had kept her half breathless since the moment she had regained consciousness.

She tensed as a door in the outer building opened and closed. Her heart stopped beating as her breath caught in her throat.

Somebody was in here with her.

Who was it? The area outside the fishbowl she was in was in darkness, making it impossible for her to see the person who had just come in.

"Hello?" she called out. She had no idea if the person could hear her through the Plexiglas or not. "Who's there?" She hated the way her voice trembled, sounding so weak and frightened.

"Don't be afraid." The voice came from someplace overhead and she realized there must be a speaker system in the ceiling. She recognized the voice and suddenly she remembered how she had come to be here.

She'd opened the door to him and before he was fully inside the motel room he'd stuck her with a needle. She'd had only seconds of consciousness before the darkness had rushed up and swallowed her.

"Gary, what have you done?" she asked.

He stepped close enough to the glass that she could now see him. It was her boss, her friend, and yet she knew now he was also her monster.

"You don't have to be afraid, Janis. I would never hurt you. I don't even want to touch you." He looked beyond her and clucked his tongue. "You've made quite a bit of a mess upending your table and moving your chairs."

She took a step closer to the glass. "Gary, if you take me back now, I won't tell anyone what you've done. Nobody has to know and we can just go on the way we were before."

"Now, why would I do that? Why would I even thing about taking you back? I've gone to a lot of trouble to make this the perfect place for you to live.

You don't have to worry about anything. You don't have to stress yourself by serving nasty men who try to touch you inappropriately. Whatever you want, I'll provide for you. All you have to do is ask."

He smiled and for the first time she thought she saw a hint of madness shining from his eyes. "This is what I dreamed of since that morning I first sat with you in the café."

"What do you want from me?" she asked in frustration...in fear.

"Nothing. I just want to have you. I want to watch you as you go about your days. I want to watch you as you sleep at night. Watching you brings me a tremendous amount of happiness, Janis."

His words chilled her to the bone. This was something different than ordinary voyeurism as she understood it. There didn't appear to be a sexual component in what Gary was describing. So what kind of madness was this?

"Just take me back, Gary," she said, trying to insert some command in her voice. "Let me out of here and take me back where I belong."

"You belong here with me," he replied.

"When did you make those holes in my room at the bar?" she asked, the fake bravado gone as her horrified fear sneaked into her voice once again.

"The day that I offered you the job at the bar and the room to live in. I knew before I left the café that day that you were going to be somebody special to me."

She sucked in a breath. My God, he'd been watching her for years and she'd never sensed anything calculating or odd from him. He'd been so incredibly normal in his madness.

"Watching you through those holes was frustrating. I could only do it at night and on Sundays." He spoke so matter-of-factly, as if his behavior was perfectly normal. "It was in the last year that I realized I needed more. I didn't want to watch you from little holes anymore. I needed something better, and so I built this place."

"What about Abigail and your children?"

"What about them? They have nothing to do with any of this. I love my wife and I adore my children. What I have with you has nothing to do with them."

"You shot Sawyer." Her mind continued to reel.

Gary nodded. "I tried to kill him. He had no business being with you. I tried to warn him off with the note and the flat tire, but that didn't work. Don't worry about him anymore. Now that I have you, I won't have to kill him. You belong to me, Janis. You have since you were nineteen. I just couldn't let another man get close to you."

"Gary, for God's sake, let me out of here. You need professional help. What you're doing isn't normal." She tried to keep her voice calm and friendly even though she wanted to leap through the glass and scratch his eyes out.

This man had violated her for years, he'd tried to

kill the man she loved, and yet he smiled at her as if she should be happy to be here in his monstrous prison.

"I don't need help. I don't care if what I'm doing isn't normal. I'm doing what makes me happy. I've finally gotten what I want. Now, you've been through a lot. It wouldn't hurt you to get some extra rest. I'll just dim the lights for you and then you can just forget I'm here." He stepped back from the glass, disappearing into the shadowed darkness.

If he thought she was going to undress and get into bed to sleep while he was there, he was out of his mind. A hysterical laugh nearly escaped her. He was out of his mind.

The overhead light dimmed but remained illuminated enough that she still couldn't see him standing in the dark outside her glass prison.

There was only one place she could go to escape his prying eyes. The pantry. She walked across the room to the wooden structure and opened the door.

It was a small room. Packages of paper towels and toilet paper took up much of the floor space. She tossed them out and then stepped inside. She pulled the door shut behind her.

She welcomed the complete darkness as she sank down to sit on the floor. At least he couldn't see her in here. In this dark, tight space she was safe from his prying eyes.

Gary's laughter sounded from someplace overhead. "I knew there would be a couple of days of adjustment for you, Janis. And that's okay. But you can't live your life in that closet. Sooner or later you'll have to come out. You'll have to come out and accept that this is your life now. Here…with me…forever."

She squeezed her eyes tightly closed, an overwhelming hopelessness sweeping through her. She had no idea where this place was located. It could be in the Bitterroot city limits or it could be miles and miles away.

Gary hadn't even been on their suspect list. He'd been a man helping them find the guilty party. How was anyone going to find her?

At least with her tucked away here, Sawyer would no longer be at risk. Sawyer. Sawyer. Her heart cried his name over and over again.

She knew he'd be going crazy, wondering what had happened to her and who might have taken her from the motel room. She knew the kinds of thoughts that were going off in his head. Had she been hurt? Was it possible she was dead?

Her heart ached with the pain she knew he must be feeling for her. If she could only blink her eyes and be back with him, back in his warm, strong arms.

But no magic would get her out of this situation. She couldn't even believe that good police work would find her here.

As the last wind of bleakness blew through her,

stealing all her hope away, she leaned her head back against the pantry door. Gary's words echoed over and over again in her head with a horrifying finality.

Here...with me...forever.

It was just after one when Cassie placed a plate with
a sandwich in front of Sawyer. "Eat," she demanded.
and the sandwich in front of her. "I don't..."

Chapter 13

It was just after one when Cassie placed a plate with
a sandwich in front of Sawyer. "Eat," she demanded.

"I can't... I'm not hungry." He was seated in the
booth, alone for the moment as Dillon dealt with an
armed robbery at the convenience store across town.

He didn't even want to be here. He wanted to
be out driving the streets, doing something active
in an attempt to find her. But somebody had to be
point man here for all the people to check in with
after searching an area of town or any abandoned
buildings.

Sawyer had requested that somebody bring him a
notebook. It was now open in front of him as he'd begun
taking notes so that searches wouldn't be doubled.

"Sawyer, you have to eat something to keep you thinking clearly," Cassie replied. "Janis needs you to stay strong."

He gave a curt nod and picked up the sandwich. He'd eat because Cassie was right, he needed to fuel his body and his mind. But the last thing he cared about was food.

He was consumed with thoughts of Janis. They no longer had any suspects. Everyone who worked at the bar had been checked and rechecked.

The only thing they could figure was that, as loose as Gary was with the keys to the bar, it was possible one had made its way to somebody who didn't work at the bar. And that meant every man in Bitterroot was a potential suspect. But with a suspect pool so big, how would they ever find the guilty party?

At the moment there were only four people in the bar. Tanner was the bartender for the day and Annie was currently seated on a stool in front of him and softly talking.

The day regulars hadn't showed up, obviously knowing their favorite drinking place had become headquarters for a missing person's case.

Gary had called Dillon earlier to let him know that he was sick and wouldn't be coming in until later that evening. Apparently he'd picked up some kind of a stomach bug.

This couldn't go on forever. They couldn't hurt

Gary's business by being here. Probably by tomorrow things would have to move to the police station.

He grimaced at the thought and lay the remaining half sandwich back on the plate. He didn't want to believe that tomorrow would come and they still wouldn't have answers.

And, as ridiculous as it sounded, moving this to the police station would only make it more real, more horrifying, than it already was.

Where? Where are you, Janis? It was the question that pounded in his head over and over again. What if she wasn't even in Bitterroot? Enough time had passed now that she could be anywhere.

It was quite possible she wasn't even in the state of Oklahoma anymore. It was equally possible that she was dead. His greatest fear was that one of his fellow cowboys would return to tell him they'd found her body.

He quickly shoved that alarming thought out of his head. He couldn't handle it right now. He needed to believe with all his heart that she was still alive and just waiting for his rescue.

Before Dillon had left on the emergency call from the convenience store, he'd interviewed Janis's mother, who had told him that she hadn't spoken to her daughter in years and if she was missing it was probably her own fault. Sawyer had never disliked a person more in his life.

He was almost grateful when Clay came in, although he knew by the expression on his friend's face that he brought nothing. He flopped into the chair next to Sawyer's. "I checked out that old barn out on the Miller property. There was nothing in it except moldy hay and rats."

Sawyer nodded and made a note on the paper before him. "How are you holding up?" Clay asked.

"I'm hanging on by a thread," Sawyer admitted. He blew out a sigh. "If she isn't in any of the abandoned buildings around town and she isn't with any of the people we have checked out, then I won't be satisfied until we do a door-to-door search for her."

"I heard about the holdup at the convenience store. I'm assuming Dillon is busy with that right now."

"Yeah. It would be nice if all the criminals in town held off doing any criminal activity until we find Janis," Sawyer replied.

"What can I do now? Where do you need me to go?"

Clay left minutes later with instructions to head out to Abe Breckinridge's ranch and, with Abe's permission, to check out several old barns and sheds on the property.

After he left, Sawyer flipped the pages of the notebook to a clean sheet. They had to be missing something. What he wanted to do was to write down everything that had happened and everyone they had spoken to from the time the bar had been spray-painted until the moment Janis had disappeared from the motel room.

He wrote frantically, his brain in a frenzy. Somehow he felt as if the answer was there, all he had to do was sort it all out. He needed to look at the chronology of things without letting his emotions get involved.

He didn't know how long he sat and wrote, but by the time he got to the moment when they'd realized Janis had been kidnapped, he had a new name and a burning fury deep in his chest.

When Dillon walked through the door, Sawyer jumped to his feet. "I think it's Gary," he said.

Dillon frowned. "Gary? Why on earth do you think he's guilty?"

"Think about it. Who had better access to plant a listening device in the smoke alarm in Janis's room than Gary? Who knew what room she was in at the motel? And isn't it convenient that Janis disappeared the day that she was coming back here to catch the Peeping Tom? You and I and Gary were the only ones who knew of our plan."

He reached out and grabbed Dillon's forearm. "It's Gary, Dillon. I feel it in my gut. He'd been under our noses all along. He's the only person here we didn't check out. We trusted him." He dropped his hand to his side. "I'm going over to his house now."

"You'll come with me," Dillon replied firmly.

Minutes later they were in Dillon's car and headed to Gary's large, two-story home on the west side of town. "I can't believe we didn't even consider him as a suspect," Sawyer said.

"That's because we both thought he was on our side. He called the staff meeting that morning after we found the peepholes. He appeared as genuinely horrified by it as we were." Dillon hit the steering wheel with his palm. "Damn it, I should have checked him out thoroughly. Best case scenario is we bust him and find Janis. The worst that can happen is that he's home and he's innocent and we both come down with the stomach flu."

Sawyer didn't reply. He stared out the window and tried to rein in the beat of his heart. Was he right about Gary or was this just another dead end?

Dillon couldn't drive fast enough for Sawyer. The closer they got to Gary's home, the more Sawyer believed in the bar owner's guilt.

Although Sawyer didn't believe Janis was inside his home where he lived with his wife and his two daughters, he did believe Gary had Janis stashed away someplace.

He didn't know if Gary owned other property or not. If he had to, he'd beat the location out of the big, beefy man. Sawyer didn't care if Gary was in his sickbed. Hell, he didn't care if the man was on his deathbed.

Damn it, he should have thought about it sooner. He should have thought about Gary when Janis had told her how Gary had taken her off the streets and offered her the room.

Dillon pulled into the driveway of the attractive home that boasted a huge wraparound porch and a stained-glass front door. Sawyer jumped out of the car, his heart actually hurting as it beat so quickly in his chest.

Dillon knocked on the front door and Abigail answered. She was a pretty woman with long, dark hair and a warm smile. "Chief…Sawyer, what can I do for you?" Her expression was one of surprise.

"We'd like to speak with Gary," Dillon said.

Her look of surprise turned into a frown. Her oldest daughter, Kayla, joined her at the door. "But…I thought he was with you," Abigail said.

"He called me early this morning and told me he had the flu and was staying home in bed," Dillon replied.

"So where is he?" Sawyer asked.

"I have no idea. He got up really early this morning and left. He told me he'd be at the bar all day. He was quite concerned about Janis."

"Do you own any other property? Someplace he might be hanging out?" Sawyer stepped closer to Abigail, close enough that he could smell the scent of rose perfume. "Abigail, this is really important."

She looked at him helplessly. "No. I can't imagine where he'd be."

"Mom, what about that piece of property he bought a couple of years ago," Kayla said.

"Oh, that," Abigail replied.

"That what? What property?" Dillon asked.

"He bought a parcel of land just outside the city limits about six or seven years ago. He hoped the town would grow up in that direction and he'd already have the land to open another bar. But, as far as I know, he hasn't done anything on that property. I haven't been out there to look at it for years."

"Where, specifically, is it?" Dillon asked.

As Dillon got the directions from Abigail, a new rise of hope filled Sawyer. Gary had lied to his wife and then he had lied to the chief of police. He obviously had something—or in this case, someone—to hide.

"What's this all about?" Abigail asked worriedly. "Is Gary in some kind of trouble for something?" Her eyes widened. "Surely you don't think he had anything to do with Janis's disappearance."

"We can't talk about anything right now," Sawyer said. "We need to go, Dillon." The urgency was back inside him. He felt as if he might jump straight out of his skin. They had the directions to the property and they needed to get there as soon as possible.

"This is it," Sawyer said to Dillon when they were back in his car and speeding down Main Street. "I feel it in my gut. Suddenly it's the only thing that makes sense."

"Don't get your hopes up too high," Dillon cautioned. "Not until we get out there and have a look around." He got on the radio and called in several men to meet them at the location.

Sawyer stared out the window and then turned to look back at Dillon. "If he's hurt her, then I'm going to kill him."

"Don't make me have to arrest you, Sawyer. You're a good man and I'd hate to see you spend the rest of your life in prison," Dillon replied. "If Gary is guilty, then let him spend the rest of his life behind bars."

Sawyer returned his gaze out the window. The full glory of spring was right around the corner. He wanted to stretch out in the grass with Janis and listen to the earth's heartbeat. He wanted to hear her laughter ride a warm breeze. More than anything, he wanted her to be back in his arms.

"We don't want to go in all hell-bent for leather," Dillon said. "If Gary is with her, we don't want a hostage situation. That wouldn't be good for anyone. We don't know exactly what he's capable of where she's concerned."

"The last thing I want to do is to do anything that might bring more harm to her." His stomach muscles knotted with a combination of fear and anticipation, with dread and with hope. Each mile they drove only tightened the knots inside him.

They left the city limits of Bitterroot. According to

Abigail, the property was about twenty minutes outside of the town. Dillon was driving fast enough they
would reach it within fifteen minutes at the most.

It was the longest fifteen minutes of Sawyer's life.
They'd driven out of town far enough that there were
no houses or buildings on either side of the road, only
pastureland that stretched for miles.

He sat straighter as they approached the location.
Set back from the road was a huge building. It appeared to be a warehouse with no windows. Gary's
van was parked in front.

Dillon flew past it. "Hey, where are you going?"
Sawyer asked. He saw the answer in a windbreak of
trees just up the road.

Dillon pulled his car in behind the trees and then
got on the radio once again. Within minutes another
patrol car holding Ben Taylor and Juan Ramirez
joined them.

They all got out of their cars.

Sawyer stared at the building, wanting nothing
more than to run as fast as he could to the door. But
he knew they had to have a plan.

It was decided that each man would go to each
side of the building and call Dillon to let him know
if there was any way inside. It was impossible to tell
from this vantage point if there were doors or windows on the two sides of the building they couldn't
see. Sawyer was assigned to the back of the building.

They approached slowly…cautiously, moving

across the pasture in crouched positions. Sawyer's heart beat so fast, so frantically, it was all he could hear pounding in his head.

What were they going to find inside? Was she still alive? Oh, God, he needed her to be alive. He reached the back of the building and was bitterly disappointed to see there were no windows or doors.

Instead of calling Dillon, he went around the corner to see Juan. On that side of the building there were also no windows or doors.

He motioned Juan to follow him around to the front of the building where Ben and Dillon stood about three feet from the door.

"This is the only way in," Dillon whispered.

"Then we go in this way." Sawyer couldn't stand it any longer. The answer to all his questions was just a doorway away. He needed to get inside now.

Dillon nodded. "We go in fast and hope the element of surprise is on our side." They all moved closer to the door. Sawyer prayed the door was unlocked, that Gary was so secure, so confident, that he wasn't a suspect, he hadn't worried about locking the door behind him.

Dillon curled his fingers around the doorknob. Every muscle in Sawyer's body tensed. Within seconds he'd know if the woman of his dreams, the woman who held his heart, was still alive.

Dillon twisted the knob and nodded, letting them know the door was unlocked. He threw open the door and Ben and Juan rushed in with Sawyer at their heels.

The three halted, momentarily stunned by what they saw. What in the hell? Sawyer's mind worked to make sense of the glass enclosure. There was no sign of Janis, but Gary was rising from a chair outside of the enclosure, his blunt features registering surprise.

Sawyer released a bellow of rage and ran toward him. He tackled him midcenter and Gary fell to the floor on his back. Sawyer jumped on top of him and began to pummel his face with his fists.

"Sawyer, that's enough." Dillon's voice pierced through the fog of rage. "We've got him, Sawyer. Janis needs you now."

When he rose from Gary, he couldn't help the sense of satisfaction he felt as he saw Gary's bloody nose and lips. Janis! He whirled around and saw her behind the glass.

She was wonderfully alive and now that the roar of anger left his head, he heard her crying his name. He rushed toward her and placed his hands on the glass. She moved her hands to his and, for just a moment, he believed he felt the warmth of her fingertips beneath his own.

He turned back to where Dillon had handcuffed Gary. "We need to get her out of there," he said.

Ben pulled his gun and aimed it at the glass.

"No!" Sawyer yelled. "The bullets might ricochet in here and kill one of us."

Gary laughed. "You'll never get her out. She's my pretty bird trapped in my cage. She's mine forever."

"Shut up," Dillon snarled. "Otherwise, I'll let Sawyer continue to beat the crap out of you."

"We're going to get you out of there," Sawyer said to Janis. "Can you hear me?"

"I can hear you," she cried. Her voice came through a speaker. "I'm so glad you're here."

Sawyer stepped back and looked at the elaborate structure.

"Sorry about the gun thing." Ben stepped up next to him. "I wasn't thinking clearly."

"No problem," Sawyer replied. "We need to find a way inside the glass… Stand back, Janis."

She stepped back from the glass and he pounded on it with his fist.

"You can't break it," Janis said. "I already tried." Her sob was audible. "I don't know how you're going to get me out of here."

"I told you, she's mine and you can't have her," Gary cried out.

"Ben, take him out to the patrol car," Dillon said.

With Gary out of the building, Dillon joined the other two. "I can't believe he went to all this trouble to build such an elaborate space."

"If he really did intend to keep her here forever, then there has to be a place where he could bring in supplies for her." Sawyer kept his gaze away from Janis. He couldn't look at her and think clearly. He couldn't stand to look at her stressed features and her tears without losing his mind.

"The pantry," she called out. "That's the only place where there has to be an entrance." She pointed to the wooden door opposite to where they all stood.

They all took off running around the inner glass enclosure. Sawyer breathed a sigh of relief to see the wood on the outside. If it was just wood keeping her inside, then Sawyer would get through it one way or another.

"It has to be a door," Sawyer said and ran his hands around the wood in an effort to find a latch or something to make it open. "We don't have time for this," he said in frustration. "I want her out now."

"I've got a hatchet in my trunk," Dillon said. He ran back around and outside.

"We're going to get you out, Janis. Stand back from the pantry. We're coming through," he said.

"I'm so glad you found me," she replied, tears still choking her voice. "I thought I was going to be here forever."

"This is definitely not where you're spending your forever," Sawyer said firmly.

By that time Dillon was back with the hatchet. He raised it to hit the wood, but Sawyer stopped him. "Please," he asked and held out his hand for the hatchet.

Sawyer wanted to be the one to break down the door. He wanted to be the one to rescue his woman.

Dillon seemed to understand his need and, with a nod, handed him the hatchet.

Sawyer swung it with all the might he possessed and then pulled it out of the wood and swung again. He attacked the door again and again. When it had been splintered enough, he yanked on the broken wood.

When he finally broke through, he still wasn't inside. Shelves of canned goods impeded his entry. He shoved them, knocking them to the floor, his only thought to get to Janis as quickly as possible.

And then he was through and she was in his arms.

Chapter 14

Sawyer's arms had never felt so good as now, when he held her tight and she wept into the crook of his neck. "He...he came to the motel room... I...I trusted him. I opened the door and then he drugged me." She spoke around her tears. "Oh, God, I've been so scared. I thought nobody would ever find me here."

"Shh, you're safe now and Gary will never be able to bother you again," Sawyer said, his voice deep and gruff with emotion.

"I can't believe he did this to me," she said and then drew deep breaths in an effort to staunch her tears of relief.

"Honey, he's a sick man and he's going to spend the rest of his life behind bars. In prison he'll have no privacy. He'll never get his life back." He tightened his arms around her. "I thought I was never going to see you again."

She raised her head and his lips claimed hers in a gentle kiss that assured her she was really safe. When the kiss ended, she stepped out of his embrace.

Dillon and Juan were walking around the enclosure, occasionally touching the glass as if still in disbelief of the world that Gary had built for himself and Janis.

"He had to have planned this for months and months," Dillon said. He pulled out his phone and began to talk pictures.

"I sat in the pantry for most of the time," she said. "It was the one place where he couldn't see me." She wrapped her arms around herself and shivered as she remembered the long hours she had sat in the dark closet.

"I'm going to get a team of men out here to process what is now a crime scene," Dillon said. "Janis, I'd like you to come back to the station with me so I can get a full statement from you."

She nodded. Now that she was safe, she just wanted all of this to be over. She wanted to go back to her motel room and figure out what to do with the rest of her life. She was also exhausted. She hadn't slept except for short nod-offs in the closet.

"I'll come with you," Sawyer said and placed his arm over her shoulder.

She leaned into him, grateful for his strength and support.

A half an hour later they were in Dillon's backseat and heading to Bitterroot. Sawyer held her hand, his big, slightly callused hands so familiar and assuring.

"This is going to kill Abigail and the children," she said. She'd always loved Gary's family and now they would all be destroyed because of her. "I don't even have words to tell them how sorry I am."

"You don't owe them an apology," Sawyer said firmly. "You were a victim in all this."

Yes, she was a victim, but she couldn't help but wonder if she had said or done something that had made Gary do what he'd done to her. Had she somehow unconsciously invited his madness into her life?

It was after ten at night when they finally walked out of the police station. She was utterly drained. "Why don't you wait here and I'll walk down to the Watering Hole and get my truck. Then I can drive you to the motel," Sawyer said.

The night air was warm and even though logically she knew any danger to her or to Sawyer was over, she didn't want to be alone for even a few minutes.

"I'll walk with you," she said. "It's only a couple of blocks."

"Are you sure?"

"Positive." She knew he would grab her hand as they walked, and he didn't disappoint her. His hand enveloped hers with warmth as they headed down the sidewalk.

"If you hadn't checked out Gary, I would have been in that fishbowl forever," she said softly.

"I wouldn't have stopped searching for you until you were found," he replied. "I just can't believe we didn't look at Gary sooner."

"I certainly didn't suspect him. He was one of the three people I trusted." She released a deep sigh. "He hid his feelings for me very well."

"I guess sometimes it's hard to tell the sane people from the insane. But look…" He pointed his finger toward the skies overhead. "The stars are all out, as if to celebrate your rescue."

She smiled but the gesture didn't quite meet her heart. She was still overwhelmed by the trauma she'd been through. She couldn't begin to explain to Sawyer or to Dillon the horror that had existed inside her from the moment she had gained consciousness until she'd heard their voices and knew she'd been rescued.

There were simply no words to speak of her terror and the fear of some kind of escalation. Would watching her eventually grow old and when that happened would Gary want to touch her? Rape her? Or would he grow tired of her altogether and kill her and bury her in a shallow grave in the middle of nowhere? And then bring another woman into his glass house?

The worst thing of all was that she couldn't talk

about her shame and the fact that she felt so dirty. A dozen showers wouldn't take away the stain of Gary peeping in on her. She couldn't scrub enough skin off to feel clean again.

When they reached the motel, they discovered her room still held the yellow-and-black crime scene tape. Officer Aaron Kelly stood guard just outside the door.

"Dillon called me," he said and pulled a motel room key out of his pocket. "Unit two is waiting for you and we moved all your personal items there."

"Thank you," she said as she took the key from him. All she wanted was to sleep and pray that her dreams weren't haunted by her horrific experience.

Once inside the room she turned to Sawyer. "Stay with me while I sleep?"

"Of course," he replied without hesitation. "You know I'm here for whatever you need."

Yes, she knew that. His copper eyes radiated a pure love that utterly humbled her. She knew if she told him that flying to France would heal her wounds, he'd have airplane tickets within ten minutes.

"Right now what I need is a long, hot shower." She opened her suitcase on the floor and pulled out her nightgown. "I'll see you in a few minutes," she said.

"I'll be waiting for you." His words were a promise that he'd always wait for her. He'd always be there for whatever she needed.

She had the water steamy hot when she stepped beneath the spray. As she lathered and rinsed and then lathered and rinsed again, she cried.

She wept away the last of her fear and the loss of a part of her she could never get back. She cried because out of a whole town full of women, Gary had chosen her. Not that she wanted any other woman to suffer what she had, but why her?

Finally she cried because she knew how much Sawyer loved her and how much she loved him. He was the man of her dreams, but she knew she could never really be the woman of his dreams.

You're nothing but a whore, a dirty little whore. A voice thundered the words inside her head, bringing with them a pain that would never be healed.

Her mother's words finally chased her out of the shower. She dried off, pulled her nightgown on and then stepped back into the motel room.

The bed had been turned down and the only light in the room was the soft illumination from the lamp on the nightstand. Sawyer was in the bed and his gaze warmed her as she ran her fingers through her damp hair and then joined him.

"Feeling better?" he asked. His voice held a wealth of caring.

"The shower was a start," she replied.

He pulled her into his arms and she laid her head on his chest, feeling the soft rise and fall of his breaths. "I imagine it's going to take some time before you can put this all behind you."

"I was afraid to sleep, afraid to do anything, knowing he was just on the other side of the glass watching me," she said. She closed her eyes as he softly stroked her hair.

"And I was so afraid for you," he replied. "But you're safe now."

Yes, she was safe and in the arms of the man who had always made her feel safe. He'd been her guardian angel from the moment Gary had painted the hateful words across the back of his building.

"It was my own fault," she said. "I'm the one who opened the motel door to him."

"You trusted him. We all trusted him." His hand paused a moment before renewing the gentle caresses through her hair. "He fooled us all, Janis. Don't beat yourself up. All the men on the Holiday Ranch didn't see the evil in Adam Benson just like all of us didn't see it in Gary."

"It's a little scary, isn't it? How evil people function so well and walk among the rest of us without showing themselves for what they really are." She shivered as she remembered the madness she'd seen in Gary's eyes after he'd captured her.

"You don't have to worry about evil people anymore," Sawyer assured her. "I'll make sure you're safe for the rest of your life."

Once again she squeezed her eyes tightly closed

as tears burned. She didn't want to cry anymore, but she knew what was coming.

Tonight she would make love with Sawyer and then she'd sleep through the night in his arms. It was a gift she was giving to herself.

But when the light of day awakened them, she intended to break things off with him. Tonight she would love him and then tomorrow she would let him go.

Sawyer awakened before dawn. He was in no hurry to leave the bed. He was spooned around Janis, her naked body warm and welcomed against his.

They had made love last night. A slow, passionate, life-affirming coming together that had sated him on so many levels. His love for her was so great— his heart was so full of that love—it almost took his breath away.

She'd not only made love with him, she'd also allowed him to stay through the night with her. Now they could really begin planning their lives together.

They'd find that home that she'd dreamed about. He'd continue to work at the Holiday Ranch and she could go to school to get the degree her father had wanted for her. Or she could be a stay-at-home wife. Whatever made her happy, that's what he wanted.

He snoozed off and on until morning light shone through the curtains and his stomach rumbled with hunger. He had eaten only half a sandwich the day before and he had no idea what Janis had eaten, if anything, while she'd been captive.

When she woke up they'd head to the café and enjoy a big, hearty breakfast and then maybe they could go house-hunting together.

At the moment she was homeless. She could stay at the motel, but a motel room wouldn't feel like home, no matter how long she stayed.

Would she want a big wedding? Was it possible after they were married for a couple of years she might decide to have a baby? Maybe his love for her would be strong enough to finally silence her mother's voice in her head. He wouldn't press her on the children issue. He could be happy with or without children. All he wanted, all he needed, was her.

She finally stirred and rolled away from him. She stretched like a kitten and then opened her eyes.

"Good morning," he said.

"Good morning." She sat up and held the sheet high enough to hide her naked breasts. "What time is it?"

He reached for his phone on the nightstand. "It's seven thirty. Did you sleep well?"

She offered him a small smile. "You know I did. I don't even think I moved."

"No nightmares?"

"Thankfully no." She shoved her hair away from her eyes.

"I was thinking that maybe when we get cleaned

up we could head to the café for some breakfast. I don't know about you, but I'm absolutely starving."

"I need a quick shower and then we'll talk." She slid out of the bed, grabbed some clothes from her suitcase on the floor and headed to the bathroom.

He frowned as she disappeared from sight. *We'll talk.* Hadn't she said something like that when he'd told her he loved her? What was there to talk about? All he'd done was suggest they go the café for breakfast.

As the shower began running in the bathroom, he got out of bed and pulled on his clothes, a bit of anxiety forming a small knot in the pit of his stomach. He told himself not to stress, that everything was fine.

How could it not be fine when they'd made love the night before and had slept in each other's arms? She just needed time to get fully awake.

He used the kitchen sink to wash his face and then finger-combed his hair. He then sat on the edge of the bed and once again picked up his phone to check to see if he'd received any messages. There were none.

He'd called each of his brother cowboys last night while Janis had been speaking to Dillon. He'd told them that Janis was safe and that he appreciated them coming out to help in her search.

Thank God Gary hadn't laid a hand on her. What he'd put her through had been bad enough, but it could have been so much worse.

He got up from the bed as she came out of the

bathroom, smelling like flowers and looking refreshed and beautiful in jeans and a light blue blouse. "So, how about breakfast at the café?"

"Actually, I'd like you to take me to the bar to get my car."

He looked at her in surprise. "Okay. Can we do that after we eat?"

"I don't want to have breakfast with you, Sawyer." Her gaze drifted to some indefinable point over his left shoulder. "I think it's time we both went our separate ways."

He stared at her. "Is this some kind of a joke?" His heart went into a tailspin.

"No, it's no joke." Her lower lip began to tremble and still she wouldn't look at him. "I don't want to be with you anymore."

"How can you say something like that after last night?" His anxiety was now big enough in his stomach that he forgot all about food.

"Last night was a final gift I gave myself." She finally met his gaze. "Last night was all about my selfish needs, but I can't let this go any longer. There's no future for you with me, Sawyer. You need to move on."

For a long moment words refused to come to him as his mind worked around the words she had just said to him. This couldn't be happening. Surely she didn't mean it. She couldn't. He knew in his heart, in his very soul, they belonged together.

"Woman, what are you doing?" he finally managed to say.

"I'm doing what's right," she replied.

"Right? How is it right for you to walk away from me when you know how much I love you, and I know how much you love me? Don't even try to pretend that you don't."

Even though she hadn't said the exact words to him, he knew she loved him. He felt it when she gazed deep into his eyes, when she reached for his hand or when they made love. She'd showed him in a million ways that she loved him. He didn't need the words to know the depth of her feelings for him.

The sheen of tears filled her eyes. "It doesn't matter how much you love me or I love you. I'm all wrong for you."

"How on earth can you be wrong for me? You're everything I want in a woman. You're everything I want in my future." He took two steps toward her but she retreated the same amount of steps from him.

"Sawyer, I've made up my mind." She folded her arms across her chest, as if denying him any access to her heart.

"You aren't thinking clearly. You've been through a terrible trauma. Give us a couple of days before you throw me away. Come and eat breakfast with me and we'll sort all this out."

"Is that your answer for everything? Do you really believe eating at the café solves anything?"

A new wave of surprise swept through him at the touch of anger that fired in her eyes. "No, I don't believe that, but I don't understand what you're doing right now."

"I'm breaking things off with you." Tears spilled down her cheeks. "I need you to move on, to find another woman you can build a future with. Find a woman who will give you the children you want."

"You could be that woman. You would make a wonderful, loving mother. Together we could be awesome parents. And if you don't want to be a mother, I don't care. All I want, all I need, is you."

"Well, you can't have me. Not anymore." She wiped at her tears and straightened her back. "I've changed my mind about you taking me to get my car. I just want you to leave now."

Once again they locked gazes and in the depths of her eyes Sawyer sought relief from the nightmare that was unfolding.

"Just tell me why," he finally said. "Why are you doing this to us?"

"Because it's what I want. Now, please go."

He walked over to the nightstand and grabbed his hat. He didn't know what else to do. He didn't know what else to say to change her mind. He was helpless in knowing how to change things around.

As he stepped outside, he squinted. He wasn't sure if the gesture was because of the bright sunshine or because of the emotion that threatened tears.

All he'd ever wanted was to find a place where he belonged with somebody who loved him. Even with all the love and support Big Cass had given to him, it hadn't filled the hole of being orphaned at fifteen. He hadn't forgotten what unconditional love felt like and he'd longed to find that same kind of love with a woman who would be by his side forever.

He'd been so sure that woman was Janis. Now his dreams were in tatters and that old hole of loneliness was back bigger than ever. How had this happened? Even as she was telling him goodbye, he'd seen the love shining from her eyes.

He'd wanted to be the man who rescued her from danger, the man who kept her safe from all evil. He'd wanted to be the man she dreamed about, the one she laughed with and loved.

While she'd been kidnapped, he'd feared losing her. The very idea had made him sick. How was it possible he had rescued her only to lose her again when she was finally safe?

Chapter 15

It was a full day and night before Janis finally managed to pull herself out of bed and stop crying. She'd cried because of the decision she'd had to make. She'd wept because she loved Sawyer with all her heart and soul, but knew that for his own good he was better off without her. She'd cried for all the love she'd never know again from him and the future they might have shared.

She even wept for the babies she wouldn't give him. He deserved babies and she hoped he'd find a woman who would give him as many as he wanted. And the thought of him being happy with anyone else made her cry yet again.

You're nothing but a selfish whore, the damnable

voice roared in her head. *You let him make love to you and spend the night. You allowed him to believe everything was all right even knowing that you were going to break his heart... A selfish whore.*

When she finally roused herself and dressed, she called Annie.

"Could you come and pick me up at the motel and take me back to the bar so I can get my car?" she asked her friend.

"I'd drive you to the moon and back. I'm just happy you're no longer in any danger. Are you ready to go now?"

"I am," Janis replied. "I'm in unit two."

"I'll be there in fifteen minutes or so," Annie replied.

Janis not only wanted to get her car, she also wanted to retrieve any personal items still in her room there. She had no idea what the future held with Gary behind bars, but she didn't want to stay in that room. She also wasn't at all sure she wanted to work at the bar...if the bar remained open.

She'd have to explore all her options. While she had a bit of a financial cushion to see her through a week or two, she didn't want to go too long without a job.

As she stood at the door waiting for Annie to arrive, she wished she were at the café enjoying breakfast with Sawyer. If she closed her eyes, she could easily imagine the brilliant shine of his copper eyes, his robust laughter that made everyone who heard it smile. In her mind's eye she could see that sensual slide of his lips that always warmed her blood.

How long would it take her to forget him? How long before the hollow wind that blew through her finally subsided? And how was she going to see him around town and not have her heart break over and over again?

She'd chosen this path and she had to remain strong. She'd survived her childhood. She'd survived Gary, and somehow she would survive this. Thankfully at that moment Annie pulled up.

She ran to her car and got into the passenger seat.

"Hey, girl." Annie greeted her with a bright smile.

"Hey, yourself," she replied. "Thanks for doing this for me."

"No problem. Is Sawyer working?" Annie pulled out of the parking lot.

"I'm assuming so, although I'm not sure. We broke up."

Annie turned her head to look at her in shock. "What happened? I thought you two were heading for a wedding."

"This is what's best for both of us and, if you don't mind, I don't want to talk about it anymore. What's the news at the bar? Is it still open?"

"The word is that the Watering Hole was in Abigail's name and she plans to keep it business as usual."

"That's a shocker, but I guess it's good news. At least we all get to keep our jobs." Janis still didn't know if she wanted to continue working there, but she was glad all the other workers wouldn't have to look for new employment.

"I still can't believe Gary was such a creep, but you should have seen Sawyer in charge of the search parties. He was in control of everyone and he was like a man possessed with the need to find you."

Even the mention of his name hurt. "I'm just glad he found me. I was afraid I'd be in that fishbowl that Gary had built forever."

By that time Annie had pulled up to her car parked in the small lot behind the bar. "Thanks, Annie. Maybe we can have lunch one day soon," she said as she got out of the car.

"Just tell me the day and as long as I'm not working, I'll be there," Annie replied.

Janis watched her drive away and then turned to the building. How she wished Sawyer was by her side when she went inside the room where Gary had peeped at her for years.

She opened the door and stepped inside. Even knowing Gary was behind bars, a chill walked up her spine as she stared at the wall that had the holes.

She tore her gaze away and instead began to gather the items she hadn't packed when she'd left the room so hastily before. She carried things back and forth to her car and each time she crossed the threshold she tried not to think about Sawyer's kisses.

The last item she carried out was her dream notebook. She still wanted to accomplish her dream of the perfect house, but she hadn't realized just how deeply she'd allowed herself to put Sawyer into those dreams until now.

She'd envisioned him sharing morning coffee with her inside that house of her imagination. In her mind's eye, he'd been there for dinner and cuddling on the sofa to watch a movie and making love in the master bedroom.

As she drove away from the bar, she mourned for everything that would never be. She grieved for the man she had sent away and the life she'd never have with him.

She'd only been back at her motel room a few minutes and was still carrying things back and forth from her car when an unfamiliar car pulled up.

Abigail got out of the driver's side. She looked like she'd aged a hundred years in the past forty-eight hours.

She walked toward Janis with her arms open wide.

Janis had thought all her tears were spent, but as Abigail pulled her into an embrace, Janis began to cry.

"I'm so sorry," she sobbed. "Please forgive me."

"There's nothing for you to be sorry for," Abigail replied, her voice choked with suppressed tears. "I came over here to tell you how sorry I am for my husband's actions and to ask for your forgiveness." She released Janis and wiped at her eyes.

"I thought maybe he was having an affair. He would disappear for hours during the day and nights. I should have known something bad was going on. I should have pulled my head out of the sand and found out what he was doing. I could have stopped all this if I'd confronted him."

"Who could have imagined what he was doing," Janis said. "I'm just so sorry that you're going through this."

"I'm going to be fine. I just hope you are," Abigail said as she straightened her shoulders.

Janis nodded. "I'll be okay."

Abigail gave her another hug. "We're strong women, Janis. We'll get through this." She stepped back. "I just wanted to let you know your job is safe. If and when you're ready to return to work, I'll welcome you back."

By the time Abigail left, Janis felt utterly wrung out. Her heart was raw and, as wrong as it was, all she really wanted was Sawyer's arms around her.

Sawyer sat on his horse and looked at the herd of cattle milling around, but his mind was filled with thoughts of Janis. Each and every moment he had spent with her was etched on his heart, imprinted on his brain.

Why? Why had she tossed him away? Why had she destroyed their love? He just didn't get it. There had been no fight, no disagreement of any kind, between them. She had slept in his arms and then had awakened and told him to get out of her life. Why?

"Did you see that?" Clay's voice penetrated Sawyer's foggy brain.

"What?"

"A thingamagoblin just ran by."

"Yeah, right," Sawyer replied dryly.

"I figured it might take something as dramatic as that to get you back to the here and now," Clay replied.

"I just don't get it, Clay. Why would she break up with me when everything was going so good?"

"Who knows why women do what they do?" Clay looked at him. "You've got it bad."

"Yeah, I do."

"And you believe she loves you?"

"I do," Sawyer answered with absolute certainty.

"Maybe you need to fight for her."

"Fight for her?" Sawyer frowned.

"Yeah, you know, send her flowers or something to let her know you aren't giving up."

Sawyer slowly nodded. Maybe he had given up way too easily. Their love was definitely worth fighting for. Both he and Clay turned their heads when they heard a horse approaching. It was Flint.

"Sawyer, Cassie wants to talk to you," he said.

"Uh-oh, you must be in trouble." Clay grinned at him.

She probably wanted to talk to him about all the time he'd taken off to safeguard Janis, he thought as he galloped back toward the stables. It was rare that Cassie called one of them on the carpet, but it did happen occasionally.

He gave his horse a quick brush-down and then left the stable and headed for the big house.

Cassie greeted him at the back door and gestured him into the kitchen. "Sit down, Sawyer." She pointed him to a chair at the table. "Would you like a cup of coffee or something else to drink?"

"No, thanks. I'm good. Cassie, I know I've been a bit absent from the ranch lately, but I assure you that won't be happening again."

"I'm glad to hear that because I need my foreman to be present to take care of business."

He stared at her. "Foreman? Me?"

"Yes, you. Sawyer, I saw how you handled Janis's disappearance. You took charge and people listened to you. Despite the turmoil you had to be going through, you remained calm and clear-thinking. That's the kind of man I need for a foreman. So, do you still want the job?"

"Absolutely," Sawyer replied. His chest swelled with pride. She'd obviously seen that he could command respect, that he could be a man who could lead.

"Brody is going to be with us for another week.

Get together with him and let him show you all the duties the job entails."

"Yes, ma'am," he replied.

The first thing he wanted to do when he stepped back outside was to call Janis and share the good news with her. And then he remembered he didn't have that right. She didn't want to hear from him anymore.

Clay's words played in his mind. Was Janis worth fighting for? Absolutely. And maybe it was time he really fight for his woman.

Janis nearly stumbled over the bouquet of flowers outside her motel room door. She'd been about to go to breakfast at the café but the sight of the pink roses nearly brought her to her knees.

There was no card, but she didn't have to question who had left them. She wanted to throw them into the trash, but she didn't. She carried them inside and put them in a glass of water. Their scent filled the air and sharpened the longing she had for Sawyer.

But pushing Sawyer away was the single most unselfish act she'd ever performed. Even though it hurt more than she could ever imagine, she'd finally done something right.

Still, it touched her heart deeply that he'd left pink roses, knowing they represented a wealth of love to her. But pink roses weren't going to change her mind about Sawyer.

The next day just before noon she stood in front of the refrigerator, trying to decide what to make herself for lunch. The night before she had gone to the grocery store and stocked up on food supplies. She needed to figure out where she was going to live. She didn't want to spend months in a motel room with her belongings packed in the boxes she'd also retrieved from the grocery store.

But she just didn't feel up to making a move quite yet. She was broken. Her mother had begun the process years before and Gary's crimes against her had perpetuated it, and her telling Sawyer goodbye had finished it.

Her spirit had been crushed and she just wasn't up to doing much of anything right now. She couldn't make any decisions yet. Time, she told herself. She just needed some time to heal and then she'd figure out what the rest of her life looked like.

A knock fell on the door. She prayed it wasn't Sawyer. She was feeling particularly vulnerable and didn't want to see him. She opened the door to see Jimmy Wakefield, an older man who worked in the kitchen at the café.

"I've got an order here for you," he said and thrust a foam container toward her.

"But I didn't order anything," she protested.

"I don't know about that. All I know was that I was told to deliver this to you and that's what I'm doing."

"Thanks, Jimmy," she said as she took the container from him.

She stepped back into her room and instantly knew by the scent what was in the container. She carried it to the small kitchen table and opened it to find crisp, seasoned french fries.

What was he doing? She sank down in a chair and closed her eyes as she fought back tears. Damn him. He was torturing her. Why couldn't he just walk away from her and leave it be?

She opened her eyes again and it was then that she noticed the address written in black marker on the inside of the lid: 1925 Oak Street.

What did it mean? There was no question that her curiosity was piqued. She picked up one of the fries and ate it as she stared at the address.

Maybe it was a house with rooms to rent. Maybe Sawyer thought it would be a good place for her to live. She wouldn't know unless she drove there to have a look.

She finished the fries and then got into her car. It would be nice if she could find a room in a house or even a converted garage or space for rent. She hadn't intended to make a move yet, mostly because she was just too mentally tired, too broken to begin the hassle of the hunt for a place.

She did trust that he'd want her in a good space and that he probably knew about what she could afford for rent. If he'd done the hunt for her, then she

was grateful. But the roses and the fries and his finding her a place to live didn't change her mind about
him. He was still better off without her. He would
always be better off without her.

She pulled up in front of 1925 Oak Street and her
breath caught in her throat. It was her dream house.
The large two-story was painted an attractive beige
with chocolate-brown trim. The wraparound porch
boasted a porch swing that was instantly inviting.

A For Sale sign stood in the yard. Why had Sawyer sent her here? Was this some kind of a cruel
trick? A glimpse of what she couldn't afford?

No. Sawyer didn't have a cruel bone in his body.
There was no way she'd believe that he'd sent her
here to somehow taunt her. Maybe the people selling
the house were interested in renting it out.

She got out of her car. She wouldn't mind peeking through the windows to get a view of the inside.
She walked up the stairs to the porch and noticed
the front door was cracked open as if in invitation.

She paused and looked behind her. There were no
other cars parked along the curb except hers. More
importantly, there was no sign of Sawyer's truck.

She opened the door a little further. "Hello?" she
called out. Her voice had a hollow ring that made her
believe the house was completely empty.

Maybe the Realtor had been here and left for lunch
and forgot to lock up. She stepped into a large foyer.
The oak floors gleamed warmly in the sunlight. A

wooden banister and stairs were to her right, but she walked past them and into a large living room.

It was just as she'd imagined it when she'd made her dream book. There was a stone fireplace and floor-to-ceiling windows. The view outside to the backyard showed a fence and a few mature trees. It was a perfect place for a dog to romp or for children to play.

The large, airy kitchen had been fully updated with granite countertops and gleaming new appliances. There was no way she could afford renting this place.

Even knowing that, she walked up the stairs. There would be two guest rooms and a large master suite. What she didn't expect was to find Sawyer standing in the master bedroom.

"What are you doing here?" she asked, almost resentful to see him so wonderfully handsome, his eyes emitting that familiar warm copper glow.

"We need to talk."

"We already talked."

"No, you talked and now it's my turn to talk," he replied. "I need to tell you that I'm not going to give you up easily. I intend to fight for us because we belong together."

"You need to give up on me now because there will never be an 'us.'" Her heart beat frantically, as if overjoyed to see him again.

Traitorous heart, she thought.

"I need some real answers from you." He took a step closer to her. "I need to know the real reasons that you don't want to live here in this house with me and have a future of me loving you every single day."

"So you're bribing me with this house? Like you've tried to do with roses and french fries?"

"Absolutely," he replied and took another step closer. "I'll do whatever I can to get you in my life for good. Now, tell me why you're being so danged hardheaded. We love each other, so why can't we be together?"

She drew in a deep breath. "I don't love you anymore."

"I believe that as much as I believe in the existence of a thingamagoblin. You love me, Janis. I know you do. I just need to know what's holding you back, what's really going on in that pretty head of yours."

"I just think you'd be better off with another woman, one who is willing to have your babies."

"That's nonsense. I already told you the baby thing isn't an issue. Janis, I want you more than I want babies." He stepped toward her again, now close enough that she could smell his familiar cologne.

Her brain told her to turn around and run. She could get back in her car and escape him, but she was pinned in place by his gaze filled with such love and longing.

"Tell me, Janis. Tell me why we can't be together."

Tears sprang to her eyes. "Because you deserve somebody better than me."

"You're the best woman I could ever find," he said softly. "Janis, you're the woman for me, the woman I want by my side as I go through life. I want your face to be the first one I see in the mornings and the last I see before I go to sleep. I want to make love with you and sleep with you in my arms."

Suddenly he was right in front of her, his body heat radiating to warm her. "Be my lover, Janis. Be my wife."

She shook her head and closed her eyes as agonizing pain ripped through her. "I can't." She opened her eyes to find her vision misted with her tears. "Don't you get it, Sawyer? I'm nothing but a dirty, selfish whore. Is that what you want for your wife?" The tears she'd fought turned into sobs of despair.

"Honey, what are you talking about?" He tried to embrace her but she spun away from him, reeling with her grief…and her shame.

"Don't you understand? My mother was right about me, after all," she cried. "I must have whorish ways for Gary to do what he did to me…to think that it was okay to do that to me. I must have somehow encouraged him. I must have done something, and that's the truth."

Sawyer yanked her up against his chest and held her tight. She fought to get out of the embrace, pounding on his broad chest with her fists, but without avail. She finally sagged against him and she continued to sob.

"Hey, hey," he said softly as he caressed a hand up and down her back.

How many times had he stroked her back, to give her strength, to give her love? As much as she loved his touch, it couldn't change what she believed.

He continued to murmur soothing words to her until her sobbing subsided to hiccupping gasps. Still he rubbed her back, bringing the magical comfort he'd always brought to her.

"Janis, now let me tell you the real truth." He didn't release his hold on her, but rather he tightened the embrace. "The truth is your mother is a selfish, jealous woman who should have never had children. She emotionally abused you for years. She should be in jail for what she did to you."

"But…but what about Gary?"

"Gary was obviously a predator and you were an easy target. You were beautiful, and a homeless, vulnerable nineteen-year-old who had no family to protect you. Janis, he didn't pick you because you had whorish ways. He chose you because you were easy. You were the perfect victim."

He released her and used his thumbs to wipe away the last of her tears. "Loving your father doesn't make you a whore, and I don't believe you could have whorish ways about you if you tried."

His coppery eyes bathed her in love. "Stop listening to whatever voices are talking in your head and listen to me. You were your mother's victim and you were Gary's through no fault of your own. Damn it, Janis, for God's sake, love yourself so you can love me. I want you to be my woman for the rest of my life."

She stared at him, wanting to believe him, simply wanting him so badly.

"You deserve the best and, as far as I'm concerned, I'm the very best man for loving you the way you deserve to be loved." He reached out and brushed a strand of hair away from her eyes. "Let love win," he whispered.

Deserve. Was it possible she really did deserve Sawyer's love? Was it possible she'd gotten it all wrong in her dream book when she'd envisioned herself alone?

She wanted to rewrite the book and add in one ginger-haired cowboy with his sexy grin and sparkling eyes. Was it possible the voices in her head were all lies? The rants of a jealous, hateful, insecure woman?

Was the answer to all this really so easy? She just needed to learn to love herself?

"Listen to my truth, Janis, and be my wife for the rest of my life," he said.

Her heart fluttered in her chest, a flutter of freedom from her painful past. She knew the truth. Deep down in her heart she knew she hadn't deserved what had happened to her. Bad things happened to good people, wasn't that the saying? And good people rose above the bad things.

"I'm a good person," she said.

"I know that." His eyes shone with love.

"And I deserve to be happy."

"I know that, too," he replied.

"You make me happy, Sawyer. I want to be your lover and your wife. I've never wanted something so much in my life."

This time when he reached for her she went willingly into his arms. His lips captured hers in a searing kiss. It tasted of sweet desire and the promise of abiding love.

When the kiss ended they remained in each other's arms. "What do you think about the house?" he asked.

"It's beautiful. It's everything I ever dreamed of," she replied.

"Good." His eyes sparkled brightly. "I'm glad you like it because I put a down payment on it earlier this morning."

She stepped back from him. "You were that confident that I would come around?"

"Hopeful," he replied. "I was that hopeful. Besides, I figured the new foreman of the Holiday Ranch needed to live in a nice house."

"Oh, Sawyer." Happiness filled her for him. "Cassie gave you the job?"

He nodded, his slightly unruly hair glistening in

the sunlight dancing through the windows. "She did, and it's all thanks to you."

Again he pulled her into his arms. "Don't you see, Janis, you make me want to be a better man. I want to be the best man I can be for you."

"And I want to be the best woman I can be for you."

Once again he kissed her and this time she tasted her future, a future filled with love and happiness with Sawyer. He was the first cowboy who had been in her bed and he would be the last.

Epilogue

They said that everyone was nervous on their wedding day, but no nerves jumped inside Sawyer as he stood in Judge Dickenson's parlor and waited for his bride-to-be to join him.

Clay stood next to him. He, along with Judge Dickenson's wife, was serving as an official witness to the simple ceremony. Janis hadn't wanted a big to-do. In fact, she'd insisted that Sawyer wear his jeans and a white shirt, but nothing more formal.

He had surprised her with a bouquet of pink roses before she had disappeared into Edna Dickenson's bedroom to finish getting ready.

"Are you sure you aren't just a little bit nervous?" Clay asked.

"Nope, not even a little bit," he replied. "I have never been more certain of anything in my entire life."

It had been a little over a month since he and Janis had moved in together in the house of her dreams. They'd shopped for furniture and slowly filled the house piece by piece, although they still had a lot to do.

Janis had gone back to work at the bar, but she now worked fewer hours.

She'd also begun seeing Dr. Ellie Martin. A psychologist in her seventies, Ellie was working with Janis on PTSD issues related to her childhood abuse and what she'd gone through with Gary.

With each day that had passed, Sawyer's love for Janis had only grown stronger. That was why he wasn't nervous now.

At the moment all he was feeling was a touch of impatience as he waited for Janis to emerge from the bedroom.

He was ready to start their married life together right now. He was eager to put the ring on her finger and say the vows that would make their bond legal in the eyes of the law. Although in the eyes of his heart, they were already bonded heart and soul.

As the bedroom door opened, Sawyer turned around and his heart leaped into his throat. She stood there, a brown-eyed angel in a short white dress, the bouquet of pink roses in her arms.

And within minutes she would be his wife.

As she started to walk toward him, he was humbled by how much he loved her and how much he knew she loved him. Tears misted his eyes as she handed her bouquet off to Edna and then faced him with eyes that shone brightly.

Later, Sawyer wouldn't be able to tell anyone about vows because the minute he reached for her hands he was lost in a haze of happiness.

The haze didn't lift until they were in his truck and headed back to their house. "Are you sorry we didn't plan some sort of reception?" he asked.

"Not at all," she replied. "I'm looking forward to a reception just for the two of us that includes eating as much of our wedding cake as we want and then hopping into our new four-poster bed."

Their wedding cake was in a box at her feet, a crème brûlée cake from the café.

"Are you sorry?" she asked. "Are you sure you aren't sorry that we didn't have a reception and included all the Holiday Ranch cowboys?"

He shot her a quick smile. "Why would I want to spend time with a bunch of rowdy cowboys when I can spend time with you all alone?"

He pulled up into the driveway. "Sit tight," he said after he'd parked. "I'll come around to get you."

He got out of the truck and hurried around to the passenger side. He opened her door and as soon as she stepped out of the truck, he swept her up in his arms.

Her laughter shot straight into his heart. She wrapped her arms around his neck and held tight as he carried her across their threshold.

A half hour later they had changed into comfy, casual clothing and were sitting at the kitchen table with the cake in front of them.

"You know we're being complete pigs," he said as he used his fork to take another mouthful of the cake. They hadn't even bothered with dishes, but instead were eating the cake right off the cardboard it had come in from the café.

"We're allowed to be pigs on our wedding day." She grinned. "'Our wedding day.' Doesn't that sound wonderful?"

"You've made me a very happy man, Janis."

"And you've made me happier than I ever dreamed possible." She set her fork down and her expression grew more serious. "I've been doing a lot of good work with Ellie."

"I'm glad. I was so proud of you for seeking some help." When she didn't pick her fork up again, he set his down. "Why do you look so serious? Is anything wrong?"

"Not at all. For the first time in my life, I feel like everything is wonderfully right. I've just been thinking about what a good mother you had and what a good father I had."

He gazed at her curiously, wondering where she

was going with the conversation. "That's true," he replied.

"So, between the two of us, we should have all the knowledge we need to be really great parents."

He stared at her intently. Her eyes were that beautiful caramel color he'd come to recognize as her inner peace and contentment. "What are you saying?"

"I want to have your babies, Sawyer."

His breath caught in the back of his throat. "Is this some kind of a wedding day whim?"

"No, it's a wedding day vow, a promise to you." Her eyes glittered. "You're going to have that family, Sawyer. We're going to have that family together. We're going to have ginger-haired children who will know how very much they are loved every day of their life."

He stared at her, this incredible woman he'd fallen in love with, the strong woman who had been through so much and yet had come out on the other side. "Oh, woman, do you have any idea what you do to me?"

She grinned at him. "Why don't we go upstairs and you can show me."

He jumped out of his chair so quickly he upended it. She giggled as he grabbed her up into his arms. Her giggles disappeared as he took her mouth with his in a kiss that spoke of his fiery desire and his love.

In return her lips tasted of crème brûlée and passion and love. She was his forever woman and they were going to live in her dream house…a house that was now his dream because she was in it. And they were going to laugh together and love and have babies and live happily ever after.

* * * * *

LET'S TALK
Romance

For exclusive extracts, competitions
and special offers, find us online:

f facebook.com/millsandboon

O @millsandboonuk

🐦 @millsandboon

Or get in touch on 0844 844 1351*

For all the latest titles coming soon, visit
millsandboon.co.uk/nextmonth

Want even more
ROMANCE?

Join our bookclub today!